HORRiD HENRY'S
Lucky Dip

Francesca Simon

HORRID HENRY'S Lucky Dip

Illustrated by Tony Ross

Orion
Children's Books

For Ava and Jesse

This collection first published in Great Britain in 2015
by Orion Children's Books
This paperback edition first published in Great Britain in 2016
by Hodder and Stoughton

1 3 5 7 9 10 8 6 4 2

A CIP catalogue record for this book
is available from the British Library.

ISBN 978 1 4440 1592 8

Printed and bound in China

The paper and board used in this book are from well-managed forests
and other responsible sources.

Orion Children's Books
An imprint of
Hachette Children's Group
Part of Hodder and Stoughton
Carmelite House
50 Victoria Embankment
London EC4Y 0DZ

An Hachette UK Company

www.hachette.co.uk
www.hachettechildrens.co.uk
www.horridhenry.co.uk

Contents

HORRID HENRY'S YEAR

HAPPY BIRTHDAY HENRY

February is my favourite month – it's my birthday, which means loads of PRESENTS!

I got Mum the perfect gift for Mother's day.

HORRiD HENRY'S
Bad Present

Ding dong.

'I'll get it!' shrieked Horrid Henry. He jumped off the sofa, pushed past Peter, ran to the door, and flung it open.

'Hi, Grandma,' said Horrid Henry. He looked at her hopefully. Yes! She was holding a huge carrier bag. Something lumpy and bumpy bulged inside. But not just any old something, like knitting or a spare jumper. Something big. Something ginormous. That meant . . . that meant . . . yippee!

Horrid Henry loved it when Grandma visited, because she often brought him a present. Mum and Dad gave really boring presents, like socks and dictionaries and games like Virtual Classroom and Name that Vegetable.

Grandma gave really great presents, like fire engines with wailing sirens, shrieking zombies with flashing lights, and once, even the Snappy Zappy Critters that Mum and Dad had said he couldn't have even if he begged for a million years.

'Where's my present?' said Horrid Henry, lunging for Grandma's bag. 'Gimme my present!'

'Don't be horrid, Henry,' said Mum, grabbing him and holding him back.

'I'm not being horrid, I just want my present,' said Henry, scowling. Why should he wait a second

longer when it was obvious Grandma had some
fantastic gift for him?

'Hi Grandma,' said Peter. 'You know you don't
need to bring me a present when you come to visit.
You're the present.'

Horrid Henry's foot longed to kick Peter into the
next room.

'Wait till after you get your present,' hissed his
head.

'Good thinking,' said his foot.

'Thank you, Peter,' said Grandma. 'Now, have
you been good boys?'

'I've been perfect,' said Peter. 'But Henry's been
horrid.'

'Have not,' said Henry.

'Have too,' said Peter. 'Henry took all my crayons and melted them on the radiator.'

'That was an accident,' said Henry. 'How was I supposed to know they would melt? And next time get out of the hammock when you're told.'

'But it was my turn,' said Peter.

'Wasn't.'

'Was, you wormy worm toad–'

'Right,' said Grandma. She reached into the bag and pulled out two gigantic dinosaurs. One Tyrannosaurus Rex was purple, the other was green.

'RAAAAAAAA,' roared one dinosaur, rearing and bucking and stretching out his blood-red claws.

'FEED ME!' bellowed the other, shaking his head and gnashing his teeth.

Horrid Henry's heart stopped. His jaw dropped. His mouth opened to speak, but no sound came out.

Two Tyrannosaur Dinosaur Roars! Only the greatest toy ever in the history of the universe! Everyone wanted one. How had Grandma found them? They'd been sold out for weeks. Moody Margaret would die of jealousy when she saw Henry's T-Rex and heard it roaring and bellowing and stomping around the garden.

'Wow,' said Horrid Henry.

'Wow,' said Perfect Peter.

Grandma smiled. 'Who wants the purple one, and who wants the green one?'

That was a thought. Which one should he choose? Which T-Rex was the best?

Horrid Henry looked at the purple dinosaur.

Hmmm, thought Henry, I do love the colour purple.

Perfect Peter looked at the purple dinosaur.

Hmmm, thought Peter, those claws are a bit scary.

Horrid Henry looked at the green dinosaur.

Oooh, thought Henry. I like those red eyes.

Perfect Peter looked at the green dinosaur.

Oooh, thought Peter, those eyes are awfully red.

Horrid Henry sneaked a peek at Peter to see which dinosaur he wanted.

Perfect Peter sneaked a peek at Henry to see which dinosaur he wanted.

Then they pounced.

'I want the purple one,' said Henry, snatching it out of Grandma's hand. 'Purple rules.'

'I want the purple one,' said Peter.

'I said it first,' said Henry. He clutched the Tyrannosaurus tightly. How could he have hesitated for a moment? What was he thinking? The purple one was best. The green one was horrible. Who ever heard of a green T-Rex anyway?

Perfect Peter didn't know what to say. Henry had said it first. But the purple Tyrannosaurus was so obviously better than the green. Its teeth were pointier. Its scales were scalier. Its big clumpy feet were so much clumpier.

'I thought it first,' whimpered Peter.

Henry snorted. 'I thought it first, and I said it first. The purple one's mine,' he said. Just wait until he showed it to the Purple Hand Gang. What a guard it would make.

Perfect Peter looked at the purple dinosaur.

Perfect Peter looked at the green dinosaur.

Couldn't he be perfect and accept the green one? The one Henry didn't want?

'But I'm obviously the best,' hissed the purple T-Rex. 'Who'd want the boring old green one? Blecccchhhh.'

'It's true, I'm not as good as the purple one,' sobbed the green dinosaur. 'The purple is for big boys, the green is for babies.'

'I want the purple one!' wailed Peter. He started to cry.

'But they're exactly the same,' said Mum. 'They're just different colours.'

'I want the purple one!' screamed Henry and Peter.

'Oh dear,' said Grandma.

'Henry, you're the eldest, let Peter have the purple one,' said Dad.

WHAT?

'NO!' said Horrid Henry. 'It's mine.' He clutched it tightly.

'He's only little,' said Mum.

'So?' said Horrid Henry. 'It's not fair. I want the purple one!'

'Give it to him, Henry,' said Dad.

'NOOOOOOOO!' screamed Henry. 'NOOOOOO!'

'I'm counting, Henry,' said Mum. 'No TV tonight
. . . no TV tomorrow . . . no TV . . .'

'NOOOO!' screamed Horrid Henry. Then he
hurled the purple dinosaur at Peter.

Henry could hardly believe what had just
happened. Just because he was the oldest, he had to
take the bad present? It was totally and utterly and
completely unfair.

'I want the purple one!'

'You know that 'I want doesn't get',' said Peter.
'Isn't that right, Mum?'

'It certainly is,' said Mum.

Horrid Henry pounced. He was a ginormous
crocodile chomping on a very chewy child.

'AAAIIIEEEEE!' screamed Peter. 'Henry bit me.'

'Don't be horrid, Henry!' shouted Mum. 'Poor Peter.'

'Serves him right!' shrieked Horrid Henry. 'You're the meanest parents in the world and I hate you.'

'Go to your room!' shouted Dad.

'No pocket money for a week!' shouted Mum.

'Fine!' screamed Horrid Henry.

Horrid Henry sat in his bedroom.

He glared at the snot-green dinosaur scowling at him from where he'd thrown it on the floor and stomped on it. He hated the colour green. He loved the colour purple. The leader of the purple hand gang deserved the purple Dinosaur Roar.

He'd make Peter swap dinosaurs if it was the last thing he did. And if Peter wouldn't swap, he'd be sorry he was born. Henry would . . . Henry could . . .

And then suddenly Horrid Henry had a wonderful, wicked idea. Why had he never thought of this before?

Perfect Peter sat in his bedroom. He smiled at the purple dinosaur as it lurched roaring around the room.

'RRRRAAAAAAAAA! RAAAAAAAAA! FEED ME!' bellowed the dinosaur.

How lucky he was to have the purple dinosaur. Purple was much better than green. It was only fair that Peter got the purple dinosaur, and Henry got

the yucky green one. After all, Peter was perfect and
Henry was horrid. Peter deserved the purple one.

Suddenly Horrid Henry burst into his bedroom.

'Mum said to stay in your room,' squealed Peter,
shoving the dinosaur under his desk and standing
guard in front of it. Henry would have to drag him
away kicking and screaming before he got his hands
on Peter's T-Rex.

'So?' said Henry.

'I'm telling on you,' said Peter.

'Go ahead,' said Henry. 'I'm telling on you,
wibble pants.'

Tell on him? Tell what?

'There's nothing to tell,' said Perfect Peter.

'Oh yes there is,' said Henry. 'I'm going to tell everyone what a mean horrid wormy toad you are, stealing the purple dinosaur when I said I wanted it first.'

Perfect Peter gasped. Horrid? Him?

'I didn't steal it,' said Peter. 'And I'm not horrid.'

'Are too.'

'Am not. I'm perfect.'

'No you're not. If you were really perfect, you wouldn't be so selfish,' said Henry.

'I'm not selfish,' whimpered Peter.

But was he being selfish keeping the purple dinosaur, when Henry wanted it so badly?

'Mum and Dad said I could have it,' said Peter weakly.

'That's 'cause they knew you'd just start crying,' said Henry. 'Actually, they're disappointed in you. I heard them.'

'What did they say?' gasped Peter.

'That you were a crybaby,' said Henry.

'I'm not a crybaby,' said Peter.

'Then why are you acting like one, crybaby?'

Could Henry be telling the truth? Mum and Dad . . . disappointed in him . . . thinking he was a baby? A selfish baby? A horrid selfish baby?

Oh no, thought Peter. Could Henry be right? Was he being horrid?

'Go on, Peter,' urged his angel. 'Give Henry the purple one. After all, they're exactly the same, just different colours.'

'Don't do it!' urged his devil.

'Why should you always be perfect? Be horrid for once.'

'Uhmm, uhmm,' said Peter.

'You know you want to do the right thing,' said Henry.

Peter did want to do the right thing.

'Okay, Henry,' said Peter. 'You can have the purple dinosaur. I'll have the green one.'

YES!!!

Slowly Perfect Peter crawled under his desk and picked up the purple dinosaur.

'Good boy, Peter,' said his angel.

'Idiot,' said his devil.

Slowly Peter held out the dinosaur to Henry. Henry grabbed it . . .

Wait. Was he crazy? Why should he swap with Henry? Henry was only trying to trick him . . .

'Give it back!' yelled Peter.

'No!' said Henry.

Peter tugged on the dinosaur's legs.

Henry tugged on the dinosaur's head.

'Gimme!'

'Gimme!'

Tug

Tug

Yank

Yank

Snaaaaap.

Riiiiiiip.

Horrid Henry looked at the twisted purple dinosaur head in his hands.

Perfect Peter looked at the broken purple dinosaur claw in his hands.

'I want the green dinosaur!' shrieked Henry and Peter.

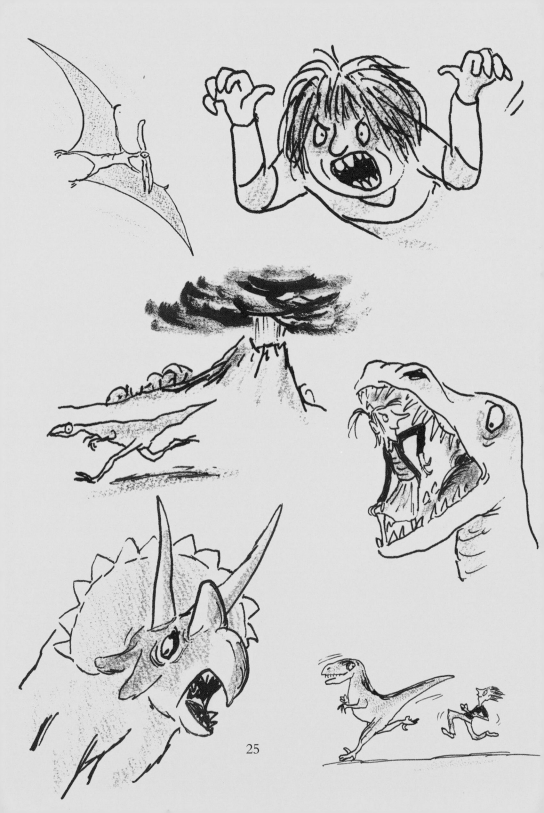

I told my wormy worm brother that Father Christmas was giving ME all his presents because he likes me best. Peter screamed and told Mum on me. So . . . while I'm stuck in my room I thought I'd write a list of the Worst Presents I've ever received, so NO ONE ever gives them to me again.

1. A lime green cardigan

2. Socks. Clothes are NOT presents

3. Rulers. School supplies are NOT presents.

4. A lunchbox (unless, of course, it has Terminator Gladiator or Mutant Max on the cover)

5. A teasy-weasy burpy slurpy doll (aaaarrrgggghhh)

6. A princess pamper parlour

7. Girl's underwear

8. Snot-green Dinosaur Roar

And here are some of the best . . .

1. Money, money, money, money, money, money

2. Mega Whirl Goo Shooter

3. Super Soaker

4. Whoopee Cushion

5. The Smellie Bellies Greatest Hits

6. Mega-gigantic TV

7. Bugle Blast Boots

HORRiD HENRY
Writes a Story

'**N**O!' screamed Horrid Henry. 'NO!'

'Don't be horrid, Henry,' said Dad.

'We'd LOVE to hear your new story, Peter,' said Mum.

'I wouldn't,' said Henry.

'Don't be rude, Henry,' said Dad.

Horrid Henry stuck his fingers in his ears and glared.

AAAARRRRRGGGGHHHHH.

Wasn't it bad enough that he had to sit at the table in front of a disgusting plate filled with – yuck – sprouts and – blecccchh – peas instead of the chips and pizza he had BEGGED Dad to cook for dinner? Did he really have to listen to Peter droning on as well?

This was torture. This was a cruel and unusual punishment. Did any child in the world ever suffer as much as Henry?

It was so unfair! Mum and Dad wouldn't let him play the Killer Boy Rats during dinner but now they wanted to force him to listen to Peter read his stupid story.

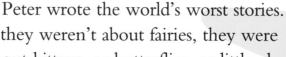 Peter wrote the world's worst stories. If they weren't about fairies, they were about kittens, or butterflies, or little elves that helped humans with their chores. His last one was all about the stupid adventures

of Peter's favourite plastic sheep, Fluff Puff, and the terrible day his pink and yellow nose turned blue. The king of the sheep had to come and wave his magic hoof to change it back . . . Henry shuddered just remembering.

And then Henry had shouted that a woodsman who really fancied a lamb chop had nabbed Fluff Puff and then Mum and Dad had sent him to his room.

Perfect Peter unfolded his piece of paper and cleared his throat.

'My story is called, *Butterfly Fairies Paint the Rainbow*,' said Peter.

'AARRGGHHH!' said Henry.

'What a lovely title,' said Mum. She glared at Henry.

'Can't wait to hear it,' said Dad. 'Stop playing with your food, Henry,' he added, as Horrid Henry started squishing peas under his knife.

'Once upon a time there lived seven butterfly fairies. There was one for every colour of the rainbow. Dance and prance, prance and dance, went the butterfly fairies every day.'

Henry groaned. 'That's just copying *Daffy and her Dancing Daisies.*'

'I'm not copying,' said Perfect Peter.

'Are too.'

'Am not.'

'Don't be horrid, Henry,' said Mum. 'Peter, that's a lovely story so far. Go on, what happens next?'

'The butterfly fairies also kept the rainbow lovely and shiny. Each fairy polished their own colour every day. But one day the butterfly fairies looked up at the sky. Whoopsydaisy! All the colours had fallen off the rainbow.'

'Call the police,' said Horrid Henry.

'Mum, Henry keeps interrupting me,' wailed Peter.

'Stop it, Henry,' said Mum.

'The fairies ran to tell their queen what had happened,' read Peter.

'"All the colours of the rainbow fell down," cried the butterfly fairies.

"Oh no."

"Oh woe."

"Boo hoo. Boo hoo.'"

SCRATCH! SCRAPE! Horrid Henry started grinding his knife into his plate.

'Stop that, Henry,' said Dad.

'I'm just eating my dinner,' said Henry. He sighed loudly. 'You're always telling me to use my knife. And now I am and you tell me to stop.'

Perfect Peter raised his voice. "'Don't cry, butterfly fairies," said the Queen. "We'll just—'"

SCRAPE!

Horrid Henry scraped louder.

'Mum!' wailed Peter. 'He's trying to ruin my story.'

'There's nothing to ruin,' said Henry.

'Be quiet, Henry,' said Dad. 'I don't want to hear another word out of you.'

Henry burped.

'Henry! I'm warning you!'

'I didn't *say* anything,' said Henry.

'Mum! I'm just getting to the really exciting bit,' said Peter. 'Henry's spoiling it.'

'Go on Peter, we're all listening,' said Mum.

"'Don't cry, butterflies," said the Queen. "We'll just have to pick up our magic paint pots and colour it back in."

"Yay," said the fairies. "Let's get to work."'

'Blecchhhhhhh!' said Horrid Henry, pretending
to vomit and knocking a few sprouts onto the
floor.

'Henry, I'm warning you . . . ' said Mum. 'Sorry,
Peter.'

'"I'll paint the rainbow blue," said blue butterfly.

"I'll paint the rainbow orange," said orange
butterfly.

"I'll paint the rainbow green," said green butterfly.

"I'll paint—"'

'"I'll paint the rainbow black and hang skulls on
it," said Terminator butterfly,' snarled Horrid Henry.

'MUM!' wailed Peter. 'Henry's interrupting me *again*!'

'Henry, this is your final warning,' said Dad. 'If I hear one more word out of you, no TV for a week.'

'Then the Fairy Queen picked up the paint pots and—'

Horrid Henry yawned loudly.

' . . . and the butterfly fairies were so happy that they began to sing:

"Tee hee. Tra la.

Tra la tra la

We are dainty little fairies

And we play and sing all day

Maybe you can come and join us

Then we'll paint the day away

Tee hee hee hee

Tra la la la."

'Blah blah, blah blah,' snarled Horrid Henry. He hadn't thought Peter could write a worse story than *The Adventures of Fluff Puff* but he was wrong.

'That's the worst story I ever heard,' said Horrid Henry.

'Henry. Be quiet,' said Dad.

Horrid Henry's fingers curled around a sprout.

'What did *you* think of my story, Mum?' said Peter.

'That was the best story I ever heard,' said Mum.

'Well done Peter,' said Dad.

Bong! A sprout hit Perfect Peter on the head.

'OW! Henry just threw a sprout at me,' wailed Peter.

'Didn't!' said Henry. 'It slipped off my fork.'

'That's it, Henry!' shouted Dad.

'Go to your room, Henry!' shouted Mum.

Horrid Henry leapt down from the table and began to stomp. 'Look at me, I'm a butterfly fairy!'

Horrid Henry stomped upstairs to his bedroom. It was so unfair. In the olden days, when people hadn't enjoyed a play, didn't they throw tomatoes and rotten oranges at the stage?

He was only being historical. Peter was lucky he
hadn't thrown much worse at him.

Well, he'd show everyone how it was done.

He'd write the greatest story ever. All about King
Hairy the Horrible and
his wicked wife
Queen Gertrude
the Gruesome.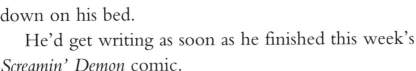
They would
spend their days
cackling and
making evil plans.

Horrid Henry lay
down on his bed.

He'd get writing as soon as he finished this week's
Screamin' Demon comic.

'Steven! Stop grunting!

William! Stop weeping!

Soraya! Stop singing!

Henry! Just stop!

Everyone. BE QUIET!' yelled Miss Battle-Axe.
She mopped her brow. One day she would retire to a
war zone and enjoy the peace and quiet.

Until then . . . she glared at her class.

'Now. I want everyone to settle down and write a story.'

Horrid Henry scowled. Miss Battle-Axe always hated his stories, even Henry's brilliant one about the Troll Werewolf Mummies who hid beneath teachers' beds and snacked on their toes. She hadn't even liked his cannibal can-can story about the cannibal dance troupe who ate their way across Europe.

It was hard, heavy work writing a story. Why should he bother when his efforts met with so little reward?

What was that stupid thing Peter had read out last night? That would do. Quickly Horrid Henry scribbled down Peter's dreadful Butterfly Fairies story. Miss Battle-Axe didn't deserve anything better.

Done! Now back to his comic. Screamin' Demon was just about to discover where the Master of the Macabre had hidden the treasure . . .

Horrid Henry felt a long fingernail poke into his shoulder. He looked up into Miss Battle-Axe's evil eye.

' . . . and why aren't you writing your story, Henry?' hissed Miss Battle-Axe.

Horrid Henry smiled.

'Because I've finished it,' said Henry.

'You . . . finished it?' said Miss Battle-Axe. She tugged on her ear. Perhaps it was time she had her earwax removed again.

'Yup,' said Henry.

'Let me see,' said Miss Battle-Axe, holding out her bony claw.

Tee hee, thought Horrid Henry, handing her the story. She doesn't believe me. Wouldn't batty old Miss Battle-Axe get a surprise.

'Hmmm,' said Miss Battle-Axe after she'd finished reading. 'Hmmm. *Butterfly Fairies Paint the Rainbow.* Hmmm.' She stared at Henry and tried to smile but her mouth had trouble turning up due to lack of practice. '*Much* better than usual, Henry.'

Henry stared. The men in white coats would be coming to take Miss Battle-Axe away any moment if she liked this story better than his others.

'In fact . . . in fact . . . I want you to go now to Miss Lovely's class and read it out loud to the Infants. They'll love it.'

What? NO!!!!!!!

Perfect Peter's class sat expectantly on the carpet as Horrid Henry stood before them, story in hand. Now everyone would think *he'd* written this stupid story. Moody Margaret would tease him until he was old and grey and toothless. But what could he do? He was trapped.

'*Putter fair pat the rainb* . . .' mumbled Horrid Henry.

'Speak up, Henry,' said Miss Lovely. 'Don't be shy. We're *so* looking forward to your story.'

'*Butterfly Fairies Paint the Rainbow*,' hissed Horrid Henry.

Perfect Peter's jaw dropped. Too late Henry realised his mistake. Writing a story about butterfly

fairies was bad enough. But he'd never hear the end
of it if people found out he'd *copied* his younger
brother's story. Though even Peter wouldn't be such
a tell-tale . . . would he?

Peter put his hand in the air.

'Miss Lovely, that's *my*—' began Peter.

'Just kidding,' said Horrid Henry hastily. 'My story
is really called, uh, *Butterfly Fairies Fight the Giants.*'

He glanced down at his story, changing words as
he read:

'Once upon a time there lived two hideous giants,
King Hairy the Horrible and Queen Gertrude the
Gruesome. Stamp and stomp, stomp and stamp went
the hideous giants every day.

They liked stomping on fairies, especially the butterfly fairies who polished the rainbow every day.

One day the giants looked up at the sky. Whoopsydaisy! All the butterfly fairies had fallen off the rainbow.

"Oh what fun," cackled King Hairy the Horrible, squishing the blue butterfly fairy.

"Yippee!" squealed Queen Gertrude the Gruesome, squashing the orange butterfly fairy.

"Ha ha!" they both shrieked, stomping on the green butterfly fairy.'

Perky Parveen looked shocked.

Spotless Sam began to sniff.

"'I'm going to roast those fairies for dinner," said Queen Gertrude the Gruesome. "Yum, yum!" she drooled, as the delicious smell of cooked fairy wafted

through the castle kitchen. Then the Queen picked up
the fairy bones and—'

Miss Lovely looked pale.

Oh no, what now, thought Horrid Henry
desperately. He'd reached Peter's horrible fairy song.

"Tee hee. Tra la.

Tra la tra la

We are dainty little fairies

And we play and sing all day

Maybe you can come and join us

Then we'll paint the day away

Tee hee hee hee

Tra la la la."

Horrid Henry took a deep breath.

'King Hairy the Horrible and Queen Gertrude
the Gruesome were so happy that they began to sing:

"Tee hee. Ha ha. Ha ha ha ha.

We are big and ugly giants

And we belch and kill all day

Maybe we can come and find you

Then we'll squish your guts away

Tee hee tee hee

Ha ha ha ha,"

bellowed Horrid Henry.

Perky Parveen began to cry.

'The fairwies got squished,' sobbed Lisping Lily.

43

'I don't want the giants to eat the fairies,' shrieked Tidy Ted.

'I'm scared,' howled Helpful Hari.

'I want my Mama,' wept Needy Neil.

'Wah!' wailed the Infants.

Horrid Henry was thrilled. What a reaction! Maybe I'll add a bit more, thought Horrid Henry. This is such a great story it's a shame to end it here.

'Let's find some bunnies,' snarled the giants. 'I'm sure—'

'Stop! Stop!' said Miss Lovely. She looked ashen. 'Better go back to your class,' she whispered. What had Miss Battle-Axe been thinking?

Horrid Henry shook his head and closed the door on the screaming, howling class.

Wow. What a great story he'd written.

Maybe he should be an author when he grew up.

Horrid Henry's Story Writing Tips

1. Nothing boring. No one wants to read a story called *My Favourite Hot Water Bottle* or *I Love My Radiator*. Remember, scary is always best. Who wouldn't want to know all about KING HENRY THE HORRIBLE or QUEEN GERTRUDE THE GRUESOME or EVIL EVIE AND THE TYRANT TEACHER.

2. Write mash-ups. Romance? Animals? Princesses? BORING!! But … why not write about an alien who falls in love with a turtle, or a vampire princess who turns into a bumble bee, or a ghost romance, or an animal sports day. Or … no, I'm keeping the best idea for me.

3. Steal good ideas. It's so much easier to copy someone else. Just do a few quick switches and – bingo! – you've written your story with loads of time left over to watch telly and eat crisps. If I could turn the worst story ever written, Peter's *Butterfly Fairies Paint the Rainbow*, into an exciting adventure about giants stomping about, so can you.

4. In fact, if you make every story all about ME you're guaranteed to write a good one.

HORRID HENRY
and the Zombie Vampire

'Isn't it exciting, Henry?' said Perfect Peter, packing Bunnykins carefully in his Sammy the Snail overnight bag. 'A museum sleepover! With a torch-lit trail! And worksheets! I can't think of anything more fun.'

'I can,' snarled Horrid Henry. Being trapped in a cave with Clever Clare reciting all the multiplication tables from one to a million. Watching *Cooking Cuties*. Even visiting Nurse Needle for one of her horrible injections. (Well, maybe not *that*).

But *almost* anything would be better than being stuck overnight in Our Town Museum on a class sleepover. No TV. No computers. No comics. Why oh why did he have to do this? He wanted to sleep in his own comfy bed, not in a sleeping bag on the museum's cold hard floor, surrounded by photos of old mayors and a few dusty exhibits.

AAARRRRGGGHH.

Wasn't it bad enough he was bored all day in school without being bored all night too?

Worse, Peter's nappy baby class was coming, too. They'd probably have to be tucked in at seven o'clock, when they'd all start crying for their mamas.

Waaaaaaaa!

Ugghh. And then Miss Battle-Axe snarling at them to finish their worksheets, and Moody Margaret snoring and Anxious Andrew whimpering that he'd seen a ghost . . .

Well, no way was he going to that boring old dump without some comics to pass the time. He'd just bought the latest *Screamin' Demon* with a big article all about vampires and zombies. Yay! He couldn't wait to read it.

Perfect Peter watched him stuff his Mutant Max bag full of comics.

'Henry, you know we're not allowed to bring comics to the museum sleepover,' said Perfect Peter.

'Shut up and mind your own business, toad,' said Horrid Henry.

'Mum! Henry just called me a toad!' wailed Peter. 'And he told me to shut up.'

'Toady Toady Toady, Toady Toady Toady,' jeered Henry.

'Henry! Stop being horrid or no museum sleepover for you,' yelled Mum.

Horrid Henry paused. Was it too late to be horrid enough to get banned from the sleepover? Why hadn't he thought of this before? Why, he could . . .

'Henry! Peter! We have to leave *now!*' yelled Dad.
Rats.

The children queued up in the museum's Central Hall
clutching their sleeping bags as Miss Lovely and Miss
Battle-Axe ticked off names on a big register.

'Go away, Susan,' said Moody Margaret. 'After
what you did at my house I'm going to sit with
Gurinder. So there.'

'You're such a meanie, Margaret,' said Sour Susan.

'Am not.'

'Are too.'

Susan scowled. Margaret was *always* so mean. If only she could think of a way to pay that old grouch back.

Margaret scowled. Susan was *always* so annoying. If only she could think of a way to pay that old fraidy cat back.

Henry scowled. Why did he have to be here? What he'd give for a magic carpet to whisk him straight home to the comfy black chair to watch *Terminator Gladiator*. Could life get any worse?

'Henwy,' came a little voice next to him. 'I love you Henwy. I want to give you a big kiss.'

Oh no, thought Horrid Henry. Oh no. It was Lisping Lily, New Nick's little sister. What was that foul fiend doing here?

'You keep away from me,' said Horrid Henry, pushing and shoving his way through the children to escape her.

'Waaa!' wept Weepy William as Henry stepped on his foot.

'I want my mama,' cried Needy Neil as Henry trampled on his sleeping bag.

'But I want to marry with you, Henwy,' lisped Lily, trying to follow him.

'Henry! Stay still!' barked Miss Battle-Axe, glaring at him with her demon eyes.

'Hello boys and girls, what an adventure we're going to have tonight,' said the museum's guide, Earnest Ella, as she handed out pencils and worksheets. Henry groaned. Boring! He hated worksheets.

'Did you know that our museum has a famous collection of balls of wool through the ages?' droned Earnest Ella. 'And an old railway car? Oh yes, it's going to be an exciting sleepover night. We're even going on a torch-lit walk through the corridors.'

Horrid Henry yawned and sneaked a peek at his comic book, which he'd hidden beneath his museum worksheet.

Horrid Henry gasped as he read *How To Recognise a Vampire* and *How to Recognise a Zombie*. Big scary teeth? Big googly eyes? Looks like the walking dead? Wow, that described Miss Battle-Axe perfectly. All they had to add was big fat carrot nose and . . .

A dark shadow loomed over him.

'I'll take that,' snapped Miss Battle-Axe, yanking the comic out of his hand. '*And* the rest.'

Huh?

He'd been so careful. How had she spotted that comic under his worksheet? And how did she know about the secret stash in his bag? Horrid Henry looked round the hall. Aha! There was Peter, pretending not to look at him. How dare that wormy worm toad tell on him? Just for that . . .

'Come along everyone, line up to collect your torches for our spooky walk,' said Earnest Ella. 'You wouldn't want to get left behind in the dark, would you?'

There was no time to lose. Horrid Henry slipped over to Peter's class and joined him in line with Tidy Ted and Goody Goody Gordon.

'Hello Peter,' said Henry sweetly.

Peter looked at him nervously. Did Henry suspect *he'd* told on him? Henry didn't *look* angry.

'Shame my comic got confiscated,' said Henry, "cause it had a list of how to tell whether anyone you know is a zombie vampire.'

'A zombie vampire?' said Tidy Ted.

'Yup,' said Henry.

'They're imaginary,' said Goody-Goody Gordon.

'That's what they'd *like* you to believe,' said Henry. 'But I've discovered some.'

'Where?' said Ted.

Horrid Henry looked around dramatically, then dropped his voice to a whisper.

54

'Two teachers at our school,' hissed Henry.

'Two *teachers?*' said Peter.

'What?' said Ted.

'You heard me. Zombie vampires. Miss Battle-Axe *and* Miss Lovely.'

'Miss *Lovely?*' gasped Peter.

'You're just making that up,' said Gordon.

'It was all in *Screamin' Demon*,' said Henry. 'That's why Miss Battle-Axe snatched my comic. To stop me finding out the truth. Listen carefully.'

Henry recited:

'How to recognise a vampire:

1. BIG HUGE SCARY TEETH.'

'If Miss Battle-Axe's fangs were any bigger she would trip over them,' said Horrid Henry.

Tidy Ted nodded. 'She *does* have big pointy teeth.'

'That doesn't prove anything,' said Peter.

'2. DRINKS BLOOD.'

Perfect Peter shook his head. 'Drinks . . . blood?'

'*Obviously* they do, just not *in front* of people,' said Horrid Henry. 'That would give away their terrible secret.'

'3. ONLY APPEARS AT NIGHT.'

'But Henry,' said Goody-Goody Gordon, 'we see Miss Battle-Axe and Miss Lovely every day at school. They *can't* be vampires.'

Henry sighed. 'Have you been paying attention? I didn't say they were *vampires*, I said they were *zombie* vampires. Being half-zombie lets them walk about in daylight.'

Perfect Peter and Goody-Goody Gordon looked at one another.

'Here's the total proof,' Henry continued.

'How to recognise a zombie:
1. LOOKS DEAD.'

'Does Miss Battle-Axe look dead? Definitely,' said Horrid Henry. 'I never saw a more dead-looking person.'

'But Henry,' said Peter. 'She's alive.'

Unfortunately, yes, thought Horrid Henry.

'Duh,' he said. 'Zombies always *seem* alive. Plus, zombies have got scary, bulging eyes like Miss Battle-Axe,' continued Henry. 'And they feed on human flesh.'

'Miss Lovely doesn't eat human flesh,' said Peter. 'She's a vegetarian.'

'A likely story,' said Henry.

'You're just trying to scare us,' said Peter.

'Don't you see?' said Henry. 'They're planning to pounce on us during the torch-lit trail.'

'I don't believe you,' said Peter.

Henry shrugged. 'Fine. Don't believe me. Just don't say I didn't warn you when Miss Lovely lurches out of the dark and BITES you!' he shrieked.

'Be quiet, Henry,' shouted Miss Battle-Axe.

'William. Stop weeping. There's nothing to be scared of. Linda! Stand up. It's not bedtime yet. Bert! Where's your torch?'

'I dunno,' said Beefy Bert.

Miss Lovely walked over and smiled at Peter.

'Looking forward to the torchlit walk?' she beamed.

Peter couldn't stop himself sneaking a peek at her teeth. *Were* they big? And sharp? Funny, he'd never noticed before how pointy two of them were . . . And was her face a bit . . . umm . . . pale?

No! Henry was just trying to trick him. Well, he wasn't going to be fooled.

'Time to go exploring,' said Earnest Ella. 'First stop on the torch-lit trail: our brand-new exhibit, *Wonderful World of Wool*. Then we'll be popping next door down the *Passage to the Past* to visit the old railway car and the Victorian shop and a Neanderthal cave. Torches on, everyone.'

Sour Susan smiled to herself. She'd just thought of the perfect revenge on Margaret for teasing her for being such a scaredy cat.

Moody Margaret smiled to herself. She'd just

thought of the perfect revenge on Susan for being so sour.

Ha ha Margaret, thought Susan.

I'll get you tonight.

Ha ha Susan, thought Margaret.

I'll get you tonight.

Ha ha Peter, thought Henry. I'll get you tonight.

'Follow me,' said Earnest Ella.

The children stampeded after her.

All except three.

When the coast was clear, Moody Margaret turned off her torch, darted into the pitch-black *Passage to the Past* hall and hid in the Neanderthal cave behind the caveman. She'd leap out at Susan when she walked past. MWAHAHAHAHAHAHA! Wouldn't that old scaredy cat get a fright.

Sour Susan turned off her torch and peeked down the *Passage to the Past* corridor. Empty. She tiptoed to the railway car and crept inside. Just wait till Margaret walked by . . .

Horrid Henry turned off his torch, crept down the *Passage to the Past*, sneaked into the Victorian shop and hid behind the rocking chair.

Tee hee. Just wait till Peter walked past. He'd— What was that?

Was it his imagination? Or did that spinning wheel in the corner of the shop . . . move?

CR—EEEK went the wheel.

It was so dark. But Henry didn't dare switch

 on his torch.

Moody Margaret looked over from the Neanderthal cave at the Victorian shop. Was it her imagination or was that rocking chair rocking back and forth?

Sour Susan looked out from the railway car. Was it her imagination or was the caveman moving?

There was a strange, scuttling noise.

What was that? thought Susan.

You know, thought Henry, this museum *is* kind of creepy at night.

And then something grabbed onto his leg.

'AAAARRRRGGHHH!' screamed Horrid Henry.

Moody Margaret heard a blood-curdling scream. Scarcely daring to breathe, Margaret peeped over the caveman's shoulder . . .

Sour Susan heard a blood-curdling scream.

Scarcely daring to breathe,
Susan peeped out from
the railway carriage . . .

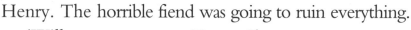

'Henwy, I found you,
Henwy,' piped the
creature clinging to his leg.

'Go away Lily,' hissed
Henry. The horrible fiend was going to ruin everything.

'Will you marry me, Henwy?'

'No!' said Horrid Henry, trying to shake her off
and brushing against the spinning wheel.

CR—EEEEK.

The spinning wheel spun.

What's that noise? thought Margaret, craning to see
from behind the caveman.

'Henwy! I want to give you a big kiss,' lisped Lily.

Horrid Henry shook his leg harder.

The spinning wheel tottered and fell over.

CRASH!

Margaret and Susan saw something lurch out of
the Victorian shop and loom up in the darkness. A
monstrous creature with four legs and waving arms . . .

'AAAARRRRGGHH!' screamed Susan.

'AAAARGGHHHHH!' shrieked Margaret.
'AAAARGGHHHHH!' shrieked Henry.

The unearthly screams rang through the museum.
Peter, Ted, and Gordon froze.

'You don't think—' gasped Gordon.

'Not . . . ' trembled Peter.

'Zombie vampires?' whimpered Ted. They
clutched one another.

'Everyone head back to the Central Hall NOW!'
shouted Earnest Ella.

In the cafeteria, Miss Lovely and Miss Battle-Axe were snatching a short break to enjoy a lovely fried egg sandwich with lashings of ketchup.

Oh my weary bones, thought Miss Battle-Axe, as she sank her teeth into the huge sandwich. Peace at last.

AAARRGGHH! EEEEEKKK! HELLLP!

Miss Battle-Axe and Miss Lovely squeezed their sandwiches in shock as they heard the terrible screams.

SPLAT!

A stream of ketchup squirted Miss Lovely in the eye and dripped down her face onto her blouse.

SQUIRT!

A blob of ketchup splatted Miss Battle-Axe on the nose and dribbled down her chin onto her cardigan.

'Sorry, Boudicca,' said Miss Lovely.

'Sorry, Lydia,' said Miss Battle-Axe.

They raced into the dark Central Hall just as their classes ran back from the torch-lit walk. Fifty beams of light from fifty torches lit up the teachers' ketchup-covered faces and ketchup-stained clothes.

'AAAARRGGHHH!' screamed Perfect Peter.

'It's the zombie vampires!' howled Tidy Ted.

'Run for your lives!' yelped Goody-Goody Gordon.

'Wait!' shouted Miss Lovely! 'Children, come back!'

'We won't eat you!' shouted Miss Battle-Axe.

'AAAARRRRGGHHHHHH!'

Pssssst. You can't be too careful. Here is my definitive list of how to tell if anyone you know is a zombie vampire.

1. Looks Dead

2. Eats Human Flesh

3. Scary Bulging Eyes

4. Big Huge Tombstone Teeth

5. Loves Bandages

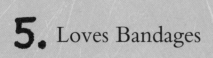

6. Hates Sunlight

7. Drinks Blood

8. Looks like the Walking Dead

9. Says MWWAAAAAAHHHAHHA a lot

10. Also says RAAAAAA and UHHHHHHRRRRGHH

What To Do If Someone You Know Turns into a Zombie Vampire.

RUN!

HORRiD HENRY'S
Invasion

'Baa! Baa! Baa!'

Perfect Peter baaed happily at his sheep collection. There they were, his ten lovely little sheepies, all beautifully lined up from biggest to smallest, heads facing forward, fluffy tails against the wall, all ten centimetres apart from one another, all—

Perfect Peter gasped. Something was wrong. Something was terribly wrong. But what? What? Peter scanned the mantelpiece. Then he saw . . .

Nooooo!

Fluff Puff, his favourite sheep, the one with the pink and yellow nose, was facing the wrong way round. His nose was shoved against the wall. His tail was facing forward. And he was . . . he was . . . crooked!

'Mum!' screamed Peter. 'Mum! Henry's been in my room again!'

'Henry!' shouted Mum. 'Keep out of Peter's room.'

'I'm not in Peter's room,' yelled Horrid Henry.
'I'm in mine.'

'But he was,' wailed Peter.

'Wasn't!' bellowed Horrid Henry.

Tee hee.

Horrid Henry was strictly forbidden to go into
Peter's bedroom without Peter's permission. But
sometimes, thought Horrid Henry, when Peter was
being even more of a toady toad than usual, he had
no choice but to invade.

Peter had run blabbing to Mum that Henry had
watched *Mutant Max* and *Knight Fight* when Mum
had said he could only watch one or the other. Henry
had been banned from watching TV all day. Peter
was such a telltale frogface ninnyhammer toady poo
bag, thought Horrid Henry grimly. Well, just wait till
Peter tried to colour in his new picture, he'd—

'MUM!' screamed Peter. 'Henry switched the caps
on my coloured pens. I just put pink in the sky.'

'Didn't!' yelled Henry.

'Did!' wailed Peter.

'Prove it,' said Horrid Henry, smirking.

Mum came upstairs. Quickly Henry leapt over the
mess covering the floor of his room, flopped on his
unmade bed and grabbed a *Screamin' Demon* comic.
Peter came and stood in the doorway.

'Henry's being horrid,' snivelled Peter.

'Henry, have you been in Peter's room?' said Mum.

Henry sighed loudly. 'Of course I've been in his smelly room. I live here, don't I?'

'I mean when he wasn't there,' said Mum.

'No,' said Horrid Henry. This wasn't a lie, because even if Peter *wasn't* there his horrible stinky smell was.

'He has too,' said Peter. 'Fluff Puff was turned the wrong way round.'

'Maybe he was just trying to escape from your pongy pants,' said Henry. '*I* would.'

'Mum!' said Peter.

'Henry! Don't be horrid. Leave your brother alone.'

'I *am* leaving him alone,' said Horrid Henry. 'Why can't he leave *me* alone? And get out of *my* room, Peter!' he shrieked, as Peter put his foot just inside Henry's door.

Peter quickly withdrew his foot.

Henry glared at Peter.

Peter glared at Henry.

Mum sighed. 'The next one who goes into the other's room without permission will be banned from the computer for a week. And no pocket money either.'

She turned to go.

Henry stuck out his tongue at Peter.

'Tell-tale,' he mouthed.

'Mum!' screamed Peter.

Perfect Peter stalked back to his bedroom. How dare Henry sneak in and mess up his sheep? What a mean, horrible brother. Perhaps he needed to calm down and listen to a little music. *The Daffy and her Dancing Daisies Greatest Hits* CD always cheered him up.

'Dance and prance! Prance and dance!

You say moo moo. We say baa.

Everybody says moo moo baa baa,' piped Perfect Peter as he put on the Daffy CD.

**Boils on your fat face
Boils make you dumb.
Chop Chop Chop 'em off
Stick 'em on your bum!**

blared the CD player.

Huh? What was that horrible song? Peter yanked out the CD. It was the Skullbangers singing the horrible 'Bony Boil' song. Henry must have sneaked a Skullbanger CD inside the Daffy case. How dare he? How dare he? Peter would storm straight downstairs and tell Mum. Henry would get into big trouble. Big big trouble.

Then Peter paused. There *was* the teeny-tiny possibility that Peter had mixed them up by mistake . . . No. He needed absolute proof of Henry's horridness. He'd do his homework, then have a good look around Henry's room to see if his Daffy CD was hidden there.

Peter glanced at his 'To Do' list pinned on his noticeboard. When he'd written it that morning it read:

Peter's To Do List
Practise cello
Fold clothes and put away
Do homework
Brush my teeth
Read Bunny's Big Boo Boo

The list now read:

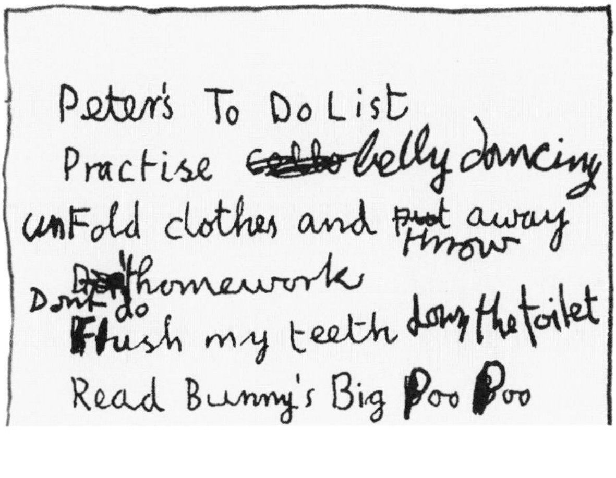

Peter's To Do List
Practise ~~cello~~ belly dancing
unFold clothes and ~~put~~ throw away
Don't do ~~Do~~ homework
~~Br~~Flush my teeth down the toilet
Read Bunny's Big Poo Poo

At the bottom someone had added:

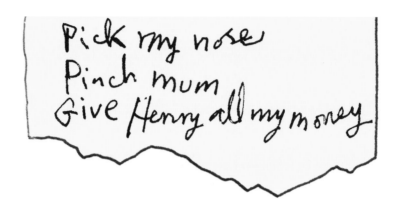

Well, here was proof! He was going to go straight down and tell on Henry.

'Mum! Henry's been in my room again. He scribbled all over my To Do list!'

'Henry!' screamed Mum. 'I am sick and tired of this! Keep out of your brother's bedroom! This is your last warning! No playing on the computer for a week!'

Sneak. Sneak. Sneak.

Horrid Henry slipped inside the enemy's bedroom. He'd pay Peter back for getting him banned from the computer.

There was Peter's cello. Ha! It was the work of a moment to unwind all the strings. Now, what else, what else? He could switch around Peter's pants and sock drawers.

No! Even better. Quickly Henry undid all of Peter's socks, and mismatched them.

Who said socks should match?

Tee hee. Peter would go mad when he found out he was wearing one Sammy the Snail sock with one Daffy sock. Then Henry snatched Bunnykins off Peter's bed and crept out.

Sneak. Sneak. Sneak.

Perfect Peter crept down the hall and stood outside Henry's bedroom, holding a muddy twig. His heart was pounding. Peter knew he was strictly forbidden to go into Henry's room without permission. But Henry kept breaking that rule. So why shouldn't he?

Squaring his shoulders, Peter tiptoed in.

Crunch.
Crunch.
Crunch.

Henry's room was a pigsty, thought Perfect Peter, wading through broken knights, crumpled sweet wrappers, dirty clothes, ripped comics, and muddy shoes.

Mr Kill. He'd steal Mr Kill. Ha! Serve Henry right. And he'd put the muddy twig in Henry's bed. Serve him double right. Perfect Peter grabbed Mr Kill, shoved the twig in Henry's bed and nipped back to his room.

And screamed.

Fluff Puff wasn't just turned the wrong way, he was— gone! Henry must have stolen him. And Lambykins was gone too. And Squish. Peter only had seven sheep left.

And where was his Bunnykins? He wasn't on the bed where he belonged. No!!!!!! This was the last straw. This was war.

The coast was clear. Peter always took ages having his bath. Horrid Henry slipped into the worm's room.

He'd pay Peter back for stealing Mr Kill. There he was, shoved at the top of Peter's wardrobe, where Peter always hid things he didn't want Henry to find. Well, ha ha ha, thought Horrid Henry, rescuing Mr Kill.

Now what to do, what to do? Horrid Henry scooped up all of Peter's remaining sheep and shoved them inside Peter's pillowcase.

What else? Henry glanced round Peter's immaculate room. He could mess it up. Nah, thought Henry. Peter loved tidying. He could— aha.

Peter had pinned drawings all over the wall above his bed. Henry surveyed them. Shame, thought

Henry, that Peter's pictures were all so dull. I mean, really, 'My Family', and 'My Bunnykins'. Horrid Henry climbed on Peter's bed to reach the drawings.

Poor Peter, thought Horrid Henry. What a terrible artist he was. No wonder he was such a smelly toad if he had to look at such awful pictures all the time. Perhaps Henry could improve them . . .

Now, let's see, thought Horrid Henry, getting out some crayons. Drawing a crown on my head would be a big improvement. There! That livens things up. And a big red nose on Peter would help, too, thought Henry, drawing away. So would a droopy moustache on Mum. And as for that stupid picture of Bunnykins, well, why not draw a lovely toilet for him to—

'What are you doing in here?' came a little voice.

Horrid Henry turned.

There was Peter, in his bunny pyjamas, glaring at him.

Uh oh. If Peter told on him again, Henry would be in big, big, mega-big trouble. Mum would probably ban him from the computer for ever.

'You're in my room. I'm telling on you,' shrieked Peter.

'Shhh!' hissed Horrid Henry.

'What do you mean, shhh?' said Peter. 'I'm going straight down to tell Mum.'

'One word and you're dead, worm,' said Horrid Henry. 'Quick! Close the door.'

Perfect Peter looked behind him.

'Why?'

'Just do it, worm,' hissed Henry.

Perfect Peter shut the door.

'What are you doing?' he demanded.

'Dusting for fingerprints,' said Horrid Henry smoothly.

Fingerprints?

'What?' said Peter.

'I thought I heard someone in your room, and ran in to check you were okay. Just look what I found,' said Horrid Henry dramatically, pointing to Peter's now empty mantelpiece.

Peter let out a squeal.

'My sheepies!' wailed Peter.

'I think there's a burglar in the house,' whispered Horrid Henry urgently. 'And I think he's hiding . . . in your room.'

Peter gulped. A burglar? In his room?

'A burglar?'

'Too right,' said Henry. 'Who do you think stole Bunnykins? And all your sheep?'

'You,' said Peter.

Horrid Henry snorted. 'No! What would I want with your stupid sheep? But a sheep rustler would love them.'

Perfect Peter hesitated. Could Henry be telling the truth? *Could* a burglar really have stolen his sheep?

'I think he's hiding under the bed,' hissed Horrid Henry. 'Why don't you check?'

Peter stepped back.

'No,' said Peter. 'I'm scared.'

'Then get out of here as quick as you can,' whispered Henry. '*I'll* check.'

'Thank you, Henry,' said Peter.

Perfect Peter crept into the hallway. Then he stopped. Something wasn't right . . . something was a little bit wrong.

Perfect Peter marched back into his bedroom. Henry was by the door.

'I think the burglar is hiding in your wardrobe, I'll get—'

'You said you were fingerprinting,' said Peter suspiciously. 'With what?'

'My fingers,' said Horrid Henry. 'Why do you think it's called *finger*printing?'

Then Peter caught sight of his drawings.

'You've ruined my pictures!' shrieked Peter.

'It wasn't me, it must have been the burglar,' said Horrid Henry.

'You're trying to trick me,' said Peter. 'I'm telling!'

Time for Plan B.

'I'm only in here 'cause you were in my room,' said Henry.

'Wasn't!'

'Were!'

'Liar!'

'Liar!'

'You stole Bunnykins!'

'You stole Mr Kill!'

'Thief!'

'Thief!'

'I'm telling on you.'

'I'm telling on you!'

Henry and Peter glared at each other.

'Okay,' said Horrid Henry. 'I won't invade your room if you won't invade mine.'

'Okay,' said Perfect Peter. He'd agree to anything to get Henry to leave his sheep alone.

Horrid Henry smirked.

He couldn't wait until tomorrow when Peter tried to play his cello . . . tee hee.

Wouldn't he get a shock!

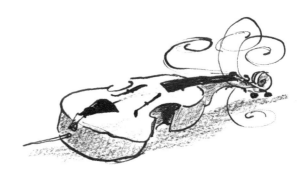

Top Tips to Stop Annoying Little Brothers and Sisters Invading Your Room

Leave your oldest, stinkiest socks, dirty clothes and empty food wrappers everywhere – your room will be so messy that not even horrible little brothers and sisters will want to come in.

Pretend there's a terrifying Fangmangler living under your bed that likes to eat younger brothers and sisters. Be sure to make scary noises every time they pass your room.

Tell them you have nits – they won't want to come anywhere near you and your creepy crawly friends!

Set up lots of booby traps – place a bucket of water over the door, make tricky tripwires out of string and set up your Goo-shooter to attack any sneaky invaders!

In case your invader manages to escape all your traps and reaches your top secret treasure drawer, place the following note inside.

You should be ashamed of yourself.

I am so disappointed that a relative of mine could be so sneaky.

Turn back before it's too late.

And never do it again!

My secret camera is filming you . . .

87

HORRID HENRY
Rocks

'Boys, I have a very special treat for you,' said Mum, beaming.

Horrid Henry looked up from his *Mutant Max* comic.

Perfect Peter looked up from his spelling homework.

A treat? A special treat? A very special treat? Maybe Mum and Dad were finally appreciating him. Maybe they'd got tickets . . . maybe they'd actually got tickets . . . Horrid Henry's heart leapt. Could it be possible that at last, at long last, he'd get to go to a Killer Boy Rats concert?

'We're going to the Daffy and her Dancing Daisies show!' said Mum. 'I got the last four tickets!'

'OOOOOOHHHH,' said Peter, clapping his hands. 'Yippee! I love Daffy.'

What?? NOOOOOOOOOOOO! That wasn't a treat. That was torture. A treat would be a day at the Frosty Freeze Ice Cream Factory. A treat would be no school. A treat would be all he could eat at Gobble and Go.

'I don't want to see that stupid Daffy,' said Horrid Henry. 'I want to see the Killer Boy Rats.'

'No way,' said Mum.

'I don't like the Killer Boy Rats,' shuddered Peter. 'Too scary.'

'Me neither,' shuddered Mum. 'Too loud.'

'Me neither,' shuddered Dad. 'Too shouty.'

'NOOOOOOOO!' screamed Henry.

'But Henry,' said Peter, 'everyone loves Daffy.'

'Not me,' snarled Henry.

Perfect Peter waved a leaflet. 'Daffy's going to be the greatest show ever. Read this.'

Daffy sings and dances her way across the stage and into your heart. Your chance to sing-along to all your favourite daisy songs! I'm a Lazy Daisy. Whoops-a-Daisy. And of course, Upsy-Daisy, Crazy Daisy, Prance and Dance-a-Daisy.

✳

With special guest star Busy Lizzie!!!

AAAAARRRRRGGGGGGHHHHHH.

Moody Margaret's parents were taking her to the Killer Boy Rats concert. Rude Ralph was going to the Killer Boy Rats concert. Even Anxious Andrew was going, and he didn't even like them. Stuck-Up

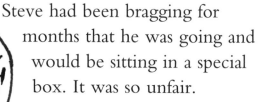

Steve had been bragging for months that he was going and would be sitting in a special box. It was so unfair.

No one was a bigger Rats fan than Horrid Henry. Henry had all their albums: Killer Boy Rats Attack-Tack-Tack, Killer Boy Rats Splat, Killer Boy Rats Manic Panic.

'It's not fair!' screamed Horrid Henry. 'I want to see the Killers!!!!'

'We have to see something that everyone in the family will like,' said Mum. 'Peter's too young for the Killer Boy Rats but we can all enjoy Daffy.'

'Not me!' screamed Henry.

Oh, why did he have such a stupid nappy baby for a brother? Younger brothers should be banned. They just wrecked everything. When he was King Henry the Horrible, all younger brothers would be arrested and dumped in a volcano.

In fact, why wait?

92

Horrid Henry pounced. He was a fiery god scooping up a human sacrifice and hurling him into the volcano's molten depths.

'AAAIIIIIEEEEEEE!' screamed Perfect Peter. 'Henry attacked me.'

'Stop being horrid, Henry!' shouted Mum. 'Leave your brother alone.'

'I won't go to Daffy,' yelled Henry. 'And you can't make me.'

'Go to your room,' said Dad.

Horrid Henry paced up and down his bedroom, singing his favourite Rats song at the top of his lungs:

I'm dead, you're dead, we're dead.
Get over it.
Dead is great, dead's where it's at
'Cause . . .

'Henry! Be quiet!' screamed Dad.

'I am being quiet!' bellowed Henry. Honestly. Now, how could he get out of going to that terrible Daffy concert? He'd easily be the oldest one there. Only stupid babies liked Daffy. If the horrible songs didn't kill him then he was sure to die of embarrassment. Then they'd be sorry they'd made him go. But it would be too late. Mum and Dad and Peter could sob and boohoo all they liked but he'd still be dead. And serve them right for being so mean to him.

Dad said if he was good he could see the Killer Boys next time they were in town. Ha. The Killer Boy Rats NEVER gave concerts. Next time they did he'd be old and hobbling and whacking Peter with his cane.

He had to get a Killer Boys ticket now. He just had to. But how? They'd been sold out for weeks.

Maybe he could place an ad:

Can you help?
Deserving Boy suffering from rare and terrible illness. His ears are falling off. Doctor has prescribed the Killer Boy Rats cure. Only by hearing the Rats live is there any hope. If you've got a ticket to the concert on Saturday PLEASE send it to Henry NOW. (If you don't you know you'll be sorry.)

That might work. Or he could tell people that the concert was cursed and anyone who went would turn into a rat. Hmmm. Somehow Henry didn't see

Margaret falling for that. Too bad Peter didn't have a ticket, thought Henry sadly, he could tell him he'd turn into a killer and Peter would hand over the ticket instantly.

And then suddenly Horrid Henry had a brilliant, spectacular idea. There must be someone out there who was desperate for a Daffy ticket. In fact there must be someone out there who would swap a Killers ticket for a Daffy one. It was certainly worth a try.

'Hey, Brian, I hear you've got a Killer Boy Rats ticket,' said Horrid Henry at school the next day.

'So?' said Brainy Brian.

'I've got a ticket to something much better,' said Henry.

'What?' said Brian. 'The Killers are the best.'

Horrid Henry could barely force the grisly words out of his mouth. He twisted his lips into a smile.

'Daffy and her Dancing Daisies,' said Horrid Henry.

Brainy Brian stared at him.

'Daffy and her Dancing Daisies?' he spluttered.

'Yes,' said Horrid Henry brightly. 'I've heard it's their best show ever. Great new songs. You'd love it.

Wanna swap?'

Brainy Brian stared at him as if he had a turnip instead of a head.

'You're trying to swap Daffy and her Dancing Daisies tickets for the Killer Boy Rats?' said Brian slowly.

'I'm doing you a favour, no one likes the Killer Boy Rats any more,' said Henry.

'I do,' said Brian.

Rats.

'How come you have a ticket for Daffy?' said Brian. 'Isn't that a baby show?'

'It's not mine, I found it,' said Horrid Henry quickly. Oops.

'Ha ha Henry, I'm seeing the Killers, and you're not!' Margaret taunted.

'Yeah Henry,' said Sour Susan.

'I heard . . .' Margaret doubled over laughing, 'I heard you were going to the Daffy show!'

'That's a big fat lie,' said Henry hotly. 'I wouldn't be seen dead there.'

Horrid Henry looked around the auditorium at the sea of little baby nappy faces. There was Needy Neil clutching his mother's hand. There was Weepy William, crying because he'd dropped his ice cream. There was Toddler Tom, up past his bedtime. Oh, no! There was Lisping Lily. Henry ducked.

Phew. She hadn't seen him. Margaret would never stop teasing him if she ever found out. When he was king, Daffy and her Dancing Daisies would live in a dungeon with only rats for company. Anyone who so much as mentioned the name Daffy, or even grew a daisy, would be flushed down the toilet.

There was a round of polite applause as Daffy and her Dancing Daisies pirouetted on stage. Horrid Henry slumped in his seat as far as he could slump and pulled his cap over his face. Thank goodness he'd

come disguised and brought some earplugs. No one would ever know he'd been.

'Tra la la la la la la!' trilled the Daisies.

'Tra la la la la la la!' trilled the audience.

Oh, the torture, groaned Horrid Henry as horrible song followed horrible song. Perfect Peter sang along. So did Mum and Dad.

AAARRRRRGGGHHHHH. And to think that tomorrow night the Killer Boy Rats would be performing . . . and he wouldn't be there! It was so unfair.

Then Daffy cartwheeled to the front of the stage. One of the daisies stood beside her holding a giant hat.

'And now the moment all you Daffy Daisy fans have been waiting for,' squealed Daffy. 'It's the Lucky Ducky Daisy Draw, when we call up on stage an oh so lucky audience member to lead us in the Whoops-a-Daisy sing-a-long song! Who's it going to be?'

'Me!' squealed Peter. Mum squeezed his arm. Daffy fumbled in the hat and pulled out a ticket. 'And the lucky winner of our ticket raffle is . . . Henry! Ticket 597! Ticket 597, yes Henry, you in row P, seat 10, come on up! Daisy needs you on stage!'

Horrid Henry was stuck to his seat in horror. It must be some other Henry. Never in his worst nightmares had he ever imagined—

'Henry, that's you,' said Perfect Peter. 'You're so lucky.'

'Henry! Come on up, Henry!' shrieked Daffy. 'Don't be shy!'

On stage at the Daffy show? No! No! Wait till Moody Margaret found out. Wait till anyone found out. Henry would never hear the end of it. He wasn't moving. Pigs would fly before he budged.

'Henwy!' squealed Lisping Lily behind him. 'Henwy! I want to give you a big kiss, Henwy . . .'

Horrid Henry leapt out of his seat. Lily! Lisping Lily! That fiend in toddler's clothing would stop at nothing to get hold of him.

Before Henry knew what had happened, ushers dressed as daisies had nabbed him and pushed him on stage.

Horrid Henry blinked in the lights. Was anyone in the world as unlucky as he?

'All together now, everyone get ready to ruffle their petals. Let's sing Tippy-toe daisy do / Let us sing a song for you!' beamed Daffy. 'Henry, you start us off.'

Horrid Henry stared at the vast audience. Everyone was looking at him. Of course he didn't know any stupid Daisy songs. He always blocked his ears or ran from the room whenever Peter sang them. Whatever could the words be . . . 'Watch out, whoop-di-do / Daisy's doing a big poo?'

These poor stupid kids. If only they could hear some decent songs, like . . . like . . .

> **'Granny on her crutches**
> **Push her off her chair**
> **Shove Shove Shove Shove**
> **Shove her down the Stairs.'**

shrieked Horrid Henry.

The audience was silent. Daffy looked stunned.

'Uh, Henry . . . that's not Tippy-toe daisy do,' whispered Daffy.

'C'mon everyone, join in with me,' shouted Horrid Henry, spinning round and twirling in his best Killer Boy Rats manner.

**'I'M IN MY COFFIN
No time for coughin'
When you're Squished down dead.**

Don't care if you're a boffin
Don't care if you're a loony,
Don't care if you're cartoony
I'll Squish you!'

sang Horrid Henry as loud as he could.

'Gonna be a rock Star (and you ain't)
Don't even—'

Two security guards ran on stage and grabbed Horrid Henry.

'Killer Boy Rats forever!' shrieked Henry, as he was dragged off.

Horrid Henry stared at the special delivery letter covered in skulls and crossbones. His hand shook.

Hey Henry,
We saw a video of you singing our songs and getting yanked off stage—way to go, killer boy! Here's a pair of tickets for our concert tonight, and a backstage pass—see you there.
The Killer Boy Rats

Horrid Henry goggled at the tickets and the backstage pass. He couldn't move. He couldn't breathe.

He was going to the Killer Boy Rats concert. He was actually going to the Killer Boy Rats concert.

Life, thought Horrid Henry, beaming, was sweet.

Horrid Henry's Best Ever Song

(Including the bits he changed and how he did it.
Learn from the master!)

"We're the smelly bellies!
We're out to get ya
Don't think we won't let ya.
Yeah Yeah Yeah
Lock up your wallets
Hide in your dungeon
'Cause a sponge will plunge in
And wipe you to death."
Oh yeah

Great lyrics!
But perhaps the last
three lines could be improved
a teensy weensy bit.

What rhymes with dungeon?
Tutankhamen!

"Hide in your dungeon
'Cause Tutankhamen
Is gonna plunge in,
And fetch ya to his
tomb!"

Perfect! True, they don't
exactly make sense, but since
when did a rock song have to
make sense? wait. wait. swap
Tutankhamen for Tutankhungeon
and the rhyme would be perfect.

"Hide in your dungeon
'Cause Tutankhungeon
Is gonna plunge in,
And fetch ya to his
tomb!"
Yeah!

After all, who knows
what those old Egyptian
hieroglyphs REALLY spell
anyway?

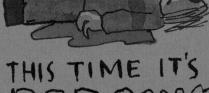

HORRID HENRY'S
Monster Movie

Horrid Henry loved scary movies. He loved nothing more than curling up on the comfy black chair with a huge bag of popcorn and a Fizzywizz drink, and jumping out of his seat in shock every few minutes. He loved wailing ghosts, oozing swamps, and bloodthirsty monsters. No film was too scary or too creepy for Horrid Henry. MWAHAHAHAHAHAHA!

Perfect Peter hated scary movies. He hated nothing more than hiding behind the comfy black chair covering his eyes and jumping out of his skin in shock every few seconds. He hated ghosts and swamps and monsters.

Even Santa Claus saying 'ho ho ho' too loudly scared him.

Thanks to Peter being the biggest scaredy-cat who ever lived, Mum and Dad would never take Henry to see any scary films.

And now, the scariest, most frightening, most terrible film ever was in town. Horrid Henry was desperate to see it.

'You're not seeing that film and that's final,' said Mum.

'Absolutely no way,' said Dad. 'Far too scary.'

'But I love scary movies!' shrieked Horrid Henry.

'I don't,' said Mum.

'I don't,' said Dad.

'I hate scary movies,' said Perfect Peter. 'Please can we see *The Big Bunny Caper* instead?'

'NO!' shrieked Horrid Henry.

'Stop shouting, Henry,' said Mum.

'But everyone's seen *The Vampire Zombie Werewolf*,' moaned Horrid Henry. 'Everyone but me.'

Moody Margaret had seen it, and said it was the best horror film ever.

Fiery Fiona had seen it three times. 'And I'm seeing it three more times,' she squealed.

Rude Ralph said he'd run screaming from the cinema.

AAAARRRRGGGGHHHHHH. Horrid Henry thought he would explode he wanted to see *The Vampire Zombie Werewolf* so much. But no. The

film came and went, and Horrid Henry wailed and gnashed.

So he couldn't believe his luck when Rude Ralph came up to him one day at playtime and said:

'I've got *The Vampire Zombie Werewolf* film on DVD. Want to come over and watch it after school?'

Did he ever!

Horrid Henry squeezed onto the sofa between Rude Ralph and Brainy Brian. Dizzy Dave sat on the floor next to Jolly Josh and Aerobic Al. Anxious Andrew sat on a chair. He'd already covered his face with his hands. Even Moody Margaret and Sour Susan were there, squabbling over who got to sit in the armchair and who had to sit on the floor.

'OK everyone, this is it,' said Rude Ralph. 'The scariest film ever. Are we ready?'

'Yeah!'

Horrid Henry gripped the sofa as the eerie piano music started.

There was a deep, dark forest.

'I'm scared!' wailed Anxious Andrew.

'Nothing's happened yet,' said Horrid Henry.

A boy and a girl ran through the shivery, shadowy trees.

'Is it safe to look?' gasped Anxious Andrew.

'Shhh,' said Moody Margaret.

'You shhh!' said Horrid Henry.

'MWAHAAAAHAAAAHAHAHAA!' bellowed Dizzy Dave.

'I'm scared!' shrieked Anxious Andrew.

'Shut up!' shouted Rude Ralph.

The pale girl stopped running and turned to the bandaged boy.

'I can't kiss you or I'll turn into a zombie,' sulked the girl.

'I can't kiss *you* or *I'll* turn into a vampire,' scowled the boy.

'But our love is so strong!' wailed the vampire girl and the zombie boy.

'Not as strong as me!' howled the werewolf, leaping out from behind a tree stump.

'AAAAAAAARRRRGGGHHH!' screeched Anxious Andrew.

'SHUT UP!' shouted Henry and Ralph.

'Leave her alone, you walking bandage,' said the werewolf.

'Leave him alone, you smelly fur ball,' said the vampire.

'This isn't scary,' said Horrid Henry.

'Shh,' said Margaret.

'Go away!' shouted the zombie.

'You go away, you big meanie,' snarled the werewolf.

'Don't you know that two's company and three's a crowd?' hissed the vampire.

'I challenge you both to an arm-wrestling contest,' howled the werewolf. 'The winner gets to keep the arms.'

'Or in your case the paws,' sniffed the vampire.

'This is the worst film I've ever seen,' said Horrid Henry.

'Shut up, Henry,' said Margaret.

'We're trying to watch,' said Susan.

'Ralph, I thought you said this was a really scary film,' hissed Henry. 'Have you *actually* seen it before?'

Rude Ralph looked at the floor.

'No,' admitted Ralph. 'But everyone said they'd seen it and I didn't want to be left out.'

'Margaret's a big fat liar too,' said Susan. 'She never saw it either.'

'Shut up, Susan!' shrieked Margaret.

'Awhoooooooo,' howled the werewolf.

Horrid Henry was disgusted. He could make a *much* scarier film. In fact . . . what was stopping him? Who better to make the scariest film of all time than Henry? How hard could it be to make a film? You just pointed a camera and yelled, 'Action!' Then he'd be rich rich rich. He'd need a spare house just to stash all his cash. And he'd be famous, too. Everyone would be begging for a role in one of his mega-horror blockbusters. *Please can we be in your new monster film?* Mum and Dad and Peter would beg. Well, they could beg as long as they liked. He'd give them his autograph, but that would be *it*.

Henry could see the poster now:

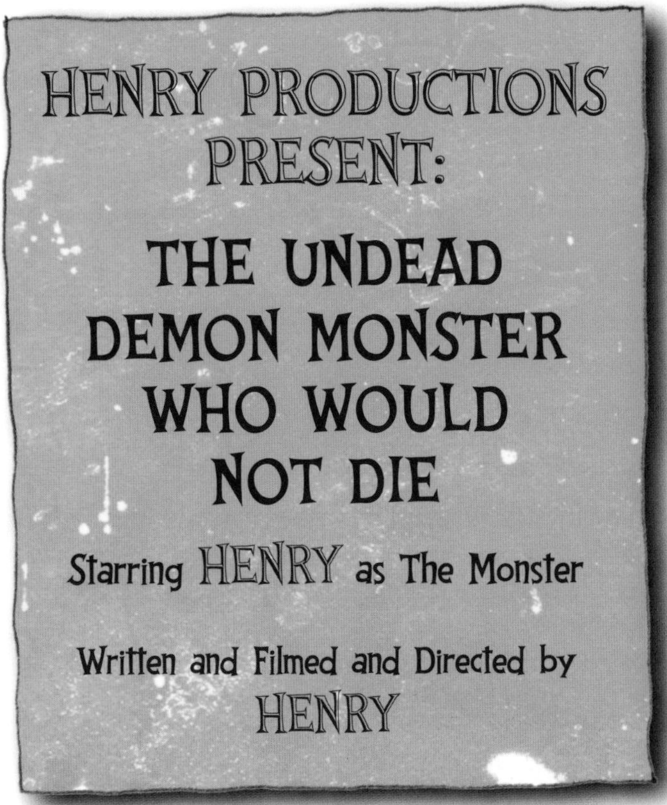

HENRY PRODUCTIONS
PRESENT:

THE UNDEAD
DEMON MONSTER
WHO WOULD
NOT DIE

Starring HENRY as The Monster

Written and Filmed and Directed by
HENRY

'I could make a *really* scary film,' said Henry.

'Not as scary as the film *I* could make,' said Margaret.

'Ha!' said Henry. 'Your scary film wouldn't scare a toddler.'

'Ha!' said Margaret. '*Your* scary film would make a baby laugh.'

'Oh yeah?' said Henry.

'Yeah,' said Margaret.

'Well, we'll just see about that,' said Henry.

Horrid Henry walked around his garden, clutching Mum's camcorder.

He could turn the garden into a swamp . . . flood a few flower beds . . . . rip up the lawn and throw buckets of mud at the windows as the monster squelched his monstrous way through the undergrowth, growling and devouring, biting and—

'Henry, can I be in your movie?' said Peter.

'No,' said Henry. 'I'm making a scary monster film. No nappy babies.'

'I am not a nappy baby,' said Peter.

'Are too.'

'Am not. Mum! Henry won't let me be in his film.'

'Henry!' yelled Mum. 'Let Peter be in your film or you can't borrow the camcorder.'

Gah! Why did everyone always get in his way? How could Henry be a great director if other people told him who to put in his film?

'Okay Peter,' said Henry, scowling. 'You can be Best Boy.'

Best Boy! That sounded super. Wow. That was a lot better than Peter had hoped.

'Best Boy!' shouted Horrid Henry. 'Get the snack table ready.'

'*Snack* table?' said Peter.

'Setting up the snack table is the most important part of making a movie,' said Henry. 'So I want biscuits and crisps and Fizzywizz drinks – NOW!' he bellowed. 'It's hungry work making a film.'

Film-making next door at Moody Margaret's house was also proceeding slowly.

'How come I have to move the furniture?' said Susan. 'You said I could *be* in your movie.'

'Because *I'm* the director,' said Margaret. 'So *I* decide.'

'Margaret, you can be the monster in *my* film. No need for any make-up,' shouted Horrid Henry over the wall.

'Shut up, Henry,' said Margaret. 'Susan. Start walking down the path.'

'BOOOOOOOOOOOOO,' shouted Horrid Henry. 'BOOOOOOOOOOOOO.'

'Cut!' yelled Margaret. 'Quiet!' she screamed. 'I'm making a movie here.'

'Peter, hold the torch and shine the spotlight on me,' ordered Henry.

'Hold the torch?' said Peter.

'It's very important,' said Henry.

'Mum said you had to let me *be* in your movie,' said Peter. 'Or I'm telling on you.'

Horrid Henry glared at Perfect Peter.

Perfect Peter glared at Horrid Henry.

'Mum!' screamed Peter.

'Okay, you can be in the movie,' said Henry.

'Stop being horrid, Henry,' shouted Mum. 'Or you hand back that camera instantly.'

'I'm not being horrid; that's in the movie,' lied Henry.

Perfect Peter opened his mouth and then closed it.

'So what's my part?' said Peter.

Perfect Peter stood on the bench in the front garden.

'Now say your line, "I am too horrible to live," and jump off the bench into the crocodile-filled moat, where you are eaten alive and drown,' said Henry.

'I don't want to say that,' said Peter.

Horrid Henry lowered the camera. 'Do you want to be in the film or don't you?' he hissed.

'I am too horrible to live,' muttered Peter.

'Louder!' said Henry.

'I am too horrible to live,' said Peter, a fraction louder.

'And as you drown, scream out, "and I have smelly pants",' said Henry.

'*What*?' said Peter.

Tee hee, thought Horrid Henry.

'But how come you get to play all the other parts, *and* dance, *and* sing, and all I get to do is walk about going wooooooo?' said Susan sourly in next door's garden.

'Because it's *my* movie,' said Margaret.

'Keep it down, we're filming here,' said Henry.
'Now Peter, you are walking down the garden path
out into the street—'

'I thought I'd just drowned,' said Peter.

Henry rolled his eyes.

'No dummy, this is a horror film. You *rose* from
the dead, and now you're walking down the path
singing this song, just before the hairy scary monster
leaps out of the bushes and rips you to shreds.

'Wibble bibble dribble pants
Bibble baby wibble pants
Wibble pants wibble pants
Dribble dribble dribble pants.'

sang Horrid Henry.

Perfect Peter hesitated. 'But Henry, why would my character sing that song?'

Henry glared at Peter.

'Because I'm the director and I say so,' said Henry.

Perfect Peter's lip trembled. He started walking.

**'Wibble bibble dribble pants
Bibble baby wibble pants
Wibble pants wib—'**

'I don't want to!' came a screech from next door's front garden.

'Susan, you *have* to be covered up in a sheet,' said Margaret.

'But no one will see my face and know it's me,' said Susan.

'Duh,' said Margaret. 'You're playing a ghost.'

Sour Susan flung off the sheet.

'Well I quit,' said Susan.

'You're fired!' shouted Margaret.

'I don't want to sing that dribble pants song,' said Peter.

'Then you're fired!' screamed Henry.

'No!' screamed Perfect Peter. 'I quit.' And he ran out of the front garden gate, shrieking and wailing.

Wow, thought Horrid Henry. He chased after Peter, filming.

'I've had it!' screamed Sour Susan. 'I don't want to be in your stupid film!' She ran off down the road, shrieking and wailing.

Margaret chased after her, filming.

Cool, thought Horrid Henry, what a perfect end for his film, the puny wimp running off terrified—

BUMP!

Susan and Peter collided and sprawled flat on the pavement.

CRASH!

Henry and Margaret tripped over the screaming Peter and Susan.

SMASH!

Horrid Henry dropped his camcorder.

SMASH!

Moody Margaret dropped *her* camcorder.

OOPS.

Horrid Henry stared down at the twisted broken metal as his monster movie lay shattered on the concrete path.

WHOOPS.

Moody Margaret stared down at the cracked camcorder as her Hollywood horror film lay in pieces on the ground.

'Henry!' hissed Margaret.

'Margaret!' hissed Henry.

...ndead Demon Monster Who Would Not Die.

Written and directed by Henry.
Reviewed by Margaret.

Gasp. Choke. Am I still alive? Have I survived watching the worst movie ever made? A film so stupid, so idiotic, so boring, that people would beg to spend 30 years in prison living on bread and water rather than have to see it a second time. This so-called horror movie is certainly a horror movie, because anyone unlucky enough to watch it will be horrified they just wasted an hour of their life. "I am too horrible to live," shouts Peter, before pretending to drown by jumping off a bench. If only the "director" had shouted the same line and followed him.

✷✷✷✷✷✷ **0 stars**

Marvellous Me.

Written and directed by Margaret.
Reviewed by Henry.

This film should be called *Ridiculous Me*. Watching the talentless Margaret sing and dance like a bellowing rhino, while Susan goes around under a sheet shrieking "Wooooooo" for some reason, is worse than having red hot pokers in your eyes.

I had to pinch myself to check I was still alive after it finally ended, as I was afraid I'd died of boredom. Margaret's singing is like listening to 1000 frogs croaking, except worse. If you had a hippo dancing and falling over that would be more graceful than Margaret stomping around. The worst film ever made, or that will ever be made.

 **0 stars**

HORRID HENRY'S
Olympics

Chomp chomp chomp chomp . . . Burp.

Ahhh! Horrid Henry scoffed the last crumb of Super Spicy Hedgehog crisps and burped again. So yummy. Wow. He'd eaten the entire pack in seventeen seconds. No one could guzzle crisps faster than Horrid Henry, especially when he was having to gobble them secretly in class. He'd never been caught, not even—

A dark, icy shadow fell across him.

'Are you eating in class, Henry?' hissed Miss Battle-Axe.

'No,' said Henry.

Tee hee. Thanks to his super-speedy jaws, he'd *already* swallowed the evidence.

'Then where did this crisp packet come from?' said Miss Battle-Axe, pointing to the plastic bag on the floor.

Henry shrugged.

'Bert! Is this yours?'

'I dunno,' said Beefy Bert.

'There is *no* eating in class,' said Miss Battle-Axe. Why did she have to say the same things over and over? One day the Queen would discover that she, Boudicca Battle-Axe, was her long-lost daughter and sweep her off to the palace, where she would live a life of pampered luxury. But until then—

130

'Now, as I was saying, before I was so rudely interrupted,' she glared at Horrid Henry, 'our school will be having its very own Olympics. We'll be running and jumping and swimming and—'

'Eating!' yelled Horrid Henry.

'Quiet, Henry,' snapped Miss Battle-Axe. 'I want all of you to practise hard, both in school and out, to show—'

Horrid Henry stopped listening. It was so unfair. Wasn't it bad enough that every morning he had to heave his heavy bones out of bed to go to school, without wasting any of his precious TV-watching time running and jumping and swimming? He was a terrible runner. He was a pathetic jumper. He was a hopeless swimmer – though he did have his five-metre badge . . . Besides, Aerobic Al was sure to win every medal. In fact they should just give them all to him now and save everyone else a load of bother.

Shame, thought Horrid Henry, that the things he was so good at never got prizes. If there was a medal for who could watch TV the longest, or who could eat the most sweets, or who was quickest out of the classroom door when the home bell rang, well, he'd be covered in gold from head to toe.

'Go on, Susan! Jump higher.'

'I'm jumping as high as I can,' said Sour Susan.

'That's not high,' said Moody Margaret. 'A tortoise could jump higher than you.'

'Then get a tortoise,' snapped Susan sourly.

'You're just a lazy lump.'

'You're just a moody meanie.'

'Lump.'

'Meanie.'

'LUMP!'

'MEANIE!'

Slap!

Slap!

'Whatcha doin'?' asked Horrid Henry, leaning over the garden wall.

'Go away, Henry,' said Margaret.

'Yeah, Henry,' said Susan.

'I can stand in my own garden if I want to,' said Henry.

'Just ignore him,' said Margaret.

'We're practising for the school Olympics,' said Susan.

Horrid Henry snorted.

'I don't see *you* practising,' said Margaret.

'That's 'cause I'm doing my *own* Olympics, frog-face,' said Henry.

His jaw dropped. YES! YES! A thousand times yes! Why hadn't he thought of this before? Of course he should set up his own Olympics. And have the competitions he'd always wanted to have. A name-calling competition! A chocolate-eating competition! A crisp-eating competition! A who-could-watch-the-most-TVs-at-the-same-time-competition! He'd make sure he had competitions that *he* could win. The Henry Olympics. The Holympics.

And the prizes would be . . .
the prizes would be . . .
masses and masses of
chocolate!

'Can Ted and Gordon and
I be in your Olympics?' said
Perfect Peter.

'NO!' said Henry. Who'd want some nappy babies
competing? They'd spoil everything, they'd—

Wait a minute . . .

'Of course you can, Peter,' said Henry smoothly.
'That will be one pound each.'

'Why?' said Ted.

'To pay for the
super fantastic prizes,
of course,' said Henry.
'Each champion will win
a massive prize of . . .
chocolate!'

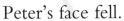

Peter's face fell.

'Oh,' he said.

'And a medal,' added Henry quickly.

'Oh,' said Peter, beaming.

'How massive?' said Margaret.

'Armfuls and armfuls,' said Horrid Henry. His
mouth watered just thinking about it.

'Hmmm,' said Margaret. 'Well, I think there should be a speed haircutting competition. And dancing.'

'Dancing?' said Henry. Well, why not? He was a brilliant dancer. His elephant stomp would win any competition hands down. 'Okay.'

Margaret and Susan plonked down one pound each.

'By the way, that's *ballroom* dancing,' said Margaret.

'No way,' said Henry.

'No ballroom dancing, then we won't enter,' said Margaret. 'And Linda and Gurinder and Kate and Fiona and Soraya won't either.'

Horrid Henry considered. He was sure to win everything else, so why not let her have a tiny victory? And the more people who entered, the more chocolate for him!

'Okay,' said Henry.

'Bet you're scared I'll win everything,' said Margaret.

'Am not.'

'Are too.'

'I can eat more sweets than you any day.'

'Ha!' said Margaret. 'I'd like to see you try.'

'The Purple Hand Gang can beat the Secret Club *and* the Best Boys Club, no sweat,' said Horrid Henry. 'Bring it on.'

THE REAL OLYMPICS ARE HERE!

TIRED OF BORING OLD SWIMMING AND RUNNING? OF COURSE YOU ARE!

NOW'S YOUR CHANCE TO COMPETE IN THE

HOLYMPICS

THE GREATEST OLYMPICS OF ALL!!!

SPEED-EATING SWEETS! TV WATCHING! CRISP EATING! BURP TO THE BEAT!

BALLROOM DANCING. SPEED HAIRCUTTING.

Entry Fee £1 for the chance to win loads of chocolate!!!!!

'Hang on,' said Margaret. 'What's with calling this the Holympics? It should be the Molympics. I came up with the haircutting and dancing competitions.'

''Cause Molympics is a terrible name,' said Henry.

'So's Holympics,' said Margaret.

'Actually,' said Peter, 'I think it should be called the Polympics.'

'Shut up, worm,' said Henry.

'Yeah, worm,' said Margaret.

'Mum!' screamed Henry. '**MUM!!!!!!!!**'

Mum came running out of the shower.

'What is it, Henry?' she said, dripping water all over the floor. 'Are you all right?'

'I need sweets,' he said.

'You got me out of the shower because you need sweets?' she repeated.

'I need to practise for the sweet speed-eating competition,' said Henry. 'For my Olympics.'

'Absolutely not,' said Mum.

Horrid Henry was outraged.

'How am I supposed to win if I can't practise?' he howled. 'You're always telling me to practise stuff. And now when I want to, you won't let me.'

Bookings for Henry's Olympics were brisk. Everyone in Henry's class – and a few from Peter's – wanted to compete. Horrid Henry gazed happily at the £45 pounds' worth of chocolate and crisps piled high on his bed. Wow. Wow. Mega mega wow. Boxes and boxes and boxes filled with yummy, yummy sweets! Giant bar after giant bar of chocolate. His Holympics would have the best prizes ever. And he, Henry, fully expected to win most of them. He'd win enough chocolate to last him a lifetime AND have the glory of coming first, for once.

Horrid Henry gazed at the chocolate prize mountain.

The chocolate prize mountain gazed back at him, and winked.

Wait.

He, Henry, was doing ALL the work. Surely it was only fair if he got *something* for his valuable time. He should have kept a bit of money back to cover his expenses.

Horrid Henry removed a giant chocolate bar from the pile.

After all, I do need to practise for the speed-eating contest, he thought, tearing off the wrapper and shoving a massive piece into his mouth. And then another. Oh boy, was that chocolate yummy. In a few seconds, it was gone.

Yeah! Horrid Henry, chocolate-eating champion of the universe!

You know, thought Henry, gazing at the chocolate mound teetering precariously on his bed, I think I bought *too* many prizes. And I *do* need to practise for my event . . .

What a great day, thought Horrid Henry happily. He'd won the sweet speed-eating competition (though Greedy Graham had come a close second), the crisp-eating contest AND the name-calling one. (Peter had run off screaming when Henry called him Wibble Wobble Pants, Nappy Noodle, and Odiferous.)

Rude Ralph won 'Burp to the Beat'. Margaret and Susan won best ballroom dancers. Vain Violet was the surprise winner of the speed haircutting competition. Weepy William . . . well, his hair would grow back – eventually.

Best of all, Aerobic Al didn't win a thing.

The winners gathered round to collect their prizes.

'Where's my chocolate, Henry?' said Moody Margaret.

'And there had better be loads like you promised,' said Vain Violet.

Horrid Henry reached into the big prize bag.

Now, where was the ballroom dancing prize?

He pulled out a Choco Bloco. Yikes, was that all the chocolate he had left? He rummaged around some more.

'A Choco Bloco?' said Margaret slowly. 'A *single* Choco Bloco?'

'They're very yummy,' said Henry.

'And mine?' said Violet.

'And mine?' said Ralph.

'And mine for coming second?' said Graham.

'You're meant to share it!' screamed Horrid Henry, as he turned and ran.

Wow, thought Horrid Henry, as he fled down the road, Rude Ralph, Moody Margaret, Sour Susan, Vain Violet, and Greedy Graham chasing after him, I'm pretty fast when I need to be. Maybe I *should* enter the school Olympics after all.

HENRY'S GOLD MEDAL SPORTS

Elephant dancing

Eating the most
Super Spicy Hedgehog
crisps in 30 seconds

watching telly

Burping to the beat

Hair chopping

Speed-eating chocolate

Name calling

HORRID HENRY'S
Nightmare

'. . . and then the slime-covered, flesh-eating zombie, fangs dripping blood, lurched into school, wailing and gnashing and – pouncing!' screamed Rude Ralph, grabbing Horrid Henry.

Henry shrieked.

'Ha ha, gotcha,' said Ralph.

Horrid Henry's heart pounded. How he loved being scared! What could be better than having a sleepover with Ralph, and both of them trying to scare the other?

He reached into the Purple Hand Fort's top secret skull and bones biscuit tin, and scoffed a big handful of chocolate gooey chewies. Scary stories and chocolate. Whoopie!

'Watch out, Ralph,' said Henry. 'I'm gonna tell you about the alien acid monster who creeps—'

'Smelly toads,' piped a little voice outside the Purple Hand Fort.

Grrr.

'Hide,' hissed Horrid Henry.

Rude Ralph belched.

'I know you're in there, Henry,' said Peter.

'No I'm not,' said Henry.

148

'And I said the password, so you have to let me in,' said Peter. 'It's my fort too. Mum said so.'

Horrid Henry sighed loudly. Why on earth, of all the possible brothers in the world, did he have to get stuck with Peter? Why oh why, when younger brothers were being distributed, did he get landed with a tell-tale, smelly nappy baby?

'All right, come in,' said Henry.

Perfect Peter crept through the branches.

'Why is it so dark in here?' said Peter.

'None of your business, baby,' said Henry. 'You've been in, now get out.'

'Yeah, wriggle off, worm,' said Ralph.

'No babies allowed in the Purple Hand Fort,' said Henry.

Perfect Peter stuck out his lower lip. 'I'm going to tell Mum you wouldn't let me stay in the fort. And that you called me a baby.'

'Go ahead, baby boo boo,' said Henry.

'MUM!' screamed Peter. 'Henry called me baby boo boo.'

'Stop being horrid, Henry, and be nice to your brother,' shouted Mum. 'Or I'll send Ralph home.'

'I wasn't being horrid,' bellowed Henry. Oh to be a wizard and turn Peter into a toadstool.

'Okay, Peter, you can stay,' snarled Henry. 'But you'll be sorry.'

'No I won't,' said Peter.

'We're telling scary stories,' said Ralph.

'And you hate scary stories,' said Henry.

Peter considered. It was true, he hated being scared. And almost everything scared him. But maybe that was last week. Maybe now that he was a week older he wouldn't be scared any more.

'I'm brave now,' said Peter.

Horrid Henry shrugged. 'Well, just don't blame me when you wake up screaming tonight,' he shrieked.

Peter jumped. Should he stay and listen to these terrible tales? Then he squared his shoulders. He wasn't a baby, whatever Henry said. He was a big boy.

Horrid Henry told his scariest story about the child-eating vampire werewolf. Rude Ralph told his scariest story about the wailing graveyard ghost who slurped up babies. Then Henry told his most scary story ever in the history of the world: the alien acid monster and zombie mummy who—

'I know a scary story,' interrupted Peter.

'We don't want to hear it,' said Henry.

'It's really scary, I promise,' said Peter. 'Once upon a time there was a bunny . . .'

'SCARY stories!' shouted Rude Ralph.

'Once upon a time there was a really big bunny,' said Peter. 'And one day his little tail fell off.'

Peter paused.

'Is that it?' said Henry.

'Yes,' said Peter.

'Blecccccchhhh,' belched Rude Ralph.

'That's your idea of a scary story?' said Henry. 'A bunny with no tail?'

'Wouldn't you be scared if you were a bunny and your tail fell off?' said Peter.

'Isn't it time for you to practise your cello?' said Henry.

Peter gasped.

He didn't ever like to miss a day's practice.

Perfect Peter trotted off.

Phew. Worm-free at last.

'Now, as I was telling you, Ralph,' said Horrid Henry, 'there was once a zombie mummy that roamed . . .'

NO!!!!!

Horrid Henry lay in bed in his dark bedroom, trembling. What a horrible, horrible nightmare. All about a ghost bunny with huge teeth and no tail, charging at him waving a gigantic needle. Ugggh. His heart was pounding so fast he thought it would pop out of his chest.

But what to do, what to do?

Henry was too scared to stay in bed. Henry was too scared to move. Don't be an idiot, snarled Devil 1. There is no such thing as a ghost bunny. Yeah, you lummox, snarled Devil 2. What a wimp. Frankly, I'm disappointed.

But Horrid Henry was too terrified to listen to reason. What if that alien acid monster or the ghost bunny was hiding under his bed? Horrid Henry wanted to lean over and check, but he couldn't.

Because what if the wailing graveyard ghost had sneaked into his wardrobe and was just waiting to GRAB him?

Worst of all, there was Ralph, snoring happily away in his sleeping bag. How could he just lie there when he was going to get gobbled up any second?

'Ralph,' hissed Henry.

'Shut up,' mumbled Ralph, rudely.

'I'm . . .' But what could Horrid Henry say? If he told Ralph he was – Horrid Henry could barely even think the word – scared, he'd never hear the end of it. Everyone would call him, Henry, leader of the Purple Hand Gang, a goochy goochy nappy baby.

Yikes.

Should he stay in bed and get eaten by the alien

acid monster, or get out of bed and get
eaten by the wailing graveyard ghost?

Actually, thought Horrid Henry,
the acid monster would get Ralph first,
since he was asleep on the floor. But if
he jumped really fast, he could race out the
door and down the hall to Mum and Dad's room
before the graveyard ghost could grab him.

But should he leave Ralph alone to face the
monsters?

Yes! thought Horrid Henry, leaping out of bed
and trampling on Rude Ralph's head.

'Uhhh,' groaned Ralph. 'Watch where you're
going, you big fat . . .'

But Horrid Henry wasn't
listening. He stampeded to
the bedroom door, dashed
into the dark hallway and
slammed the door behind him.

Right now he was so scared he didn't care if he was
too old to jump into Mum and Dad's bed.

Phew. Horrid Henry paused, gasping for breath.

He was safe. The monsters would be too busy
chomping on Ralph to nab him.

But wait. Could the graveyard ghost ooze under
the door and grab him in the hall? Worse, was the
injection bunny gliding up the stairs?

Horrid Henry froze. Oh no. His heart was
pounding.

He opened his mouth to shriek 'MUM!'

Then he closed it.

Wait a minute. Wait a minute.

Peter was sure to be awake, after all the
horrible scary stories he'd heard today. After
all, Peter was the biggest scaredy-cat ever.
If Henry was scared, Peter would be a
dripping wreck.

He'd just drop in. Seeing Peter
terrified would make him feel a whole
lot better, and a whole lot braver.

I'll bet Peter's lying there shaking and too scared to move, thought Horrid Henry. Ha. Ha. Ha.

Horrid Henry crept into Peter's room and shut the door. Then he tip-toed over to Peter's bed . . .

Huh?

There was Peter, sound asleep, a sweet smile on his face, his peaceful face lit up by his bunny nightlight and ceiling stars.

Horrid Henry's jaw dropped. How could Peter not be having horrible nightmares too? It was so unfair! He was the brave one, scared of nothing

(except injections) and Peter was the wormy worm
wibble pants noodle-head who was scared of Rudy
the Rootin-Tootin Rooster cartoon, Santa Claus, and
probably the Tooth Fairy.

Well, he'd do something about that.

'Slimy acid monster,' murmured Henry in
Peter's ear. 'Coming to get you with his great
big googly eyes and great big monster teeth. Be
afraid, Peter. Be very afraid.
OOOOOOOOOOOOHHH.'

Perfect Peter smiled in his
sleep.

'Hello Mr Monster,'
he said.

'BOO!' said
Horrid Henry.
'BOOO!'

'Would you
like a cup of tea?'
murmured Peter.

'No,'
growled Horrid
Henry. 'I want
to eat YOU!'

'Okay,' said
Peter drowsily.

What was wrong
with him? thought
Horrid Henry.
'**Mwaahahaha-
hahaha**,' cackled
Horrid Henry. **'I'm
the graveyard ghost
come to GET ya**.'

'That's nice,'
murmured Peter.

'No, it's not
nice,' growled Horrid
Henry.
'It's scary. It's terrible.
Wooooooooooo!
Arrrrggghhhhh!
BOOOOOOOOOOOOOOOOO!'

Suddenly Peter's door opened.

'AAAAAAAARRRRGGGHHH!' screamed
Horrid Henry.

'AAAAAAAARRRRGGGHHH!' screamed
Perfect Peter.

'What are you doing in here, Henry?' said Mum.

'It's 3 o'clock in the morning,' said Dad.

Horrid Henry was never so happy to see anyone
in his life.

'I thought Peter would be scared, so I came in to check on him,' said Horrid Henry.

Mum stared at Henry.

'And why did you think Peter would be scared?' asked Mum. She looked suspiciously at Henry.

''Cause I just did,' said Henry.

'Go back to your room, Henry,' said Mum.

His room? His haunted horrible room where all the monsters were lurking?

'Mum, could you just come with me?' said Henry. 'I need you to check on something.'

'Can't it wait till morning?' said Dad, yawning.

'No,' said Horrid Henry. 'I think there's a tarantula under my bed. Could you check please?'

After all, if Mum saw an acid alien there instead of a tarantula, she'd probably mention it.

Mum sighed, walked him to his room and checked under the bed.

'There's nothing there,' said Mum.

'Oh, and in my wardrobe, I'm sure I saw a . . . umm . . . mouse run in,' said Henry. 'That's what woke me. Could you just check for me?'

Mum looked in the wardrobe.

'That's it, Henry,' snapped Mum. 'Now go to sleep.'

Horrid Henry climbed back into bed and sighed happily. His room looked just as friendly and familiar as usual.

Why on earth had he been scared?

'Pssst, Ralph, you awake?' hissed Henry.

'Yeah,' said Rude Ralph, sitting up.

'Wanna hear a scary story?' said Henry. 'I know a

161

great one about a mouldering monster and a cursed
monkey paw . . .'

'Yeah!' said Rude Ralph.

HORRiD HENRY'S SUPER-SECRET PURPLE HAND FORT PASSWORDS

wibble Pants   Nappy baby

Bibble

Frog-Face   Terminator

Mr Kill

Noodle Head   Nunga

HORRiD HENRY'S
Mother's Day

'**W**hat are you doing for Mother's Day?' asked Perfect Peter.

Horrid Henry ignored him and continued to read his *Screamin' Demon* comic.

'I'm getting Mum flowers *and* chocolates *and* making her breakfast in bed,' said Peter.

Horrid Henry scowled and slumped lower on the sofa.

'What presents are *you* getting her, Henry?' asked Peter.

'None!' bellowed Horrid Henry. 'Now shut up and go away.'

'Dad!' wailed Peter. 'Henry told me to shut up.'

'Don't be horrid, Henry,' said Dad. 'Or no TV tonight.'

But Horrid Henry didn't care. Mother's Day. Oh no. Not again.

Horrid Henry hated Mother's Day.

Last year Peter gave Mum a giant hand-painted card covered in sparkles and glitter which had taken him weeks to make.

Last year Henry also made Mum a card. Okay, so he'd folded over a piece of paper and scrawled 'Happy Mother's Day' on it. Was it his fault that the

paper he'd picked up off the floor had an advert on the other side for a new kebab shop opening down the road? He'd been busy. He'd made her a card, hadn't he? Wasn't it the thought that counted?

But no. Mum was never satisfied.

Then Peter bought her a massive bouquet of red roses so Henry picked some tulips from the garden and got told off. It was so unfair.

Grrr. Aaaarrgh. Why didn't they ever celebrate Children's Day, that's what he wanted to know. Then Mum and Dad could serve *him* breakfast in bed and buy *him* presents and make *him* cards. In fact, when Henry became King he'd make it the law that every day was Children's Day and Mother's Day and Father's Day would be banned. Any parent trying to force their child to celebrate this horrible day would be buried headfirst in quicksand.

Naturally, Horrid Henry hadn't bought Mum a present. He'd been so busy watching TV and reading comics and playing on the computer and dragging his

weary bones to school and back again that there just
hadn't been any time. And Mum and Dad were so
mean and horrid and gave him the puniest amount of
pocket money ever in the history of the universe so
how could he be expected to *buy* a present out of the
few measly pence he had rattling round his skeleton
bank? He couldn't and that was that. If Mum and
Dad wanted presents from him they should give him
more cash.

Maybe Mum would forget about Mother's Day,
thought Horrid Henry hopefully. She was getting old,
after all, and didn't old people forget stuff?

'Well, boys,' said Mum, 'I'm really looking forward to Mother's Day tomorrow. I can't wait to be pampered like a queen.'

'You will be, Mum,' said Perfect Peter. 'I promise.'

Rats.

Rats. Rats. Rats. Rats. Rats.

If only Peter weren't such a goody goody wormy worm toady toad. Once again, Peter would put Henry to shame with his gifts and his cards and running to put a cushion on Mum's chair and making her breakfast in bed and . . .

Wait a minute.

Wait a minute.

Who said Peter had to outdo him this year? What if he, Henry, made Peter look horrid for once? What if, instead of *ignoring* Mother's Day, Henry made tomorrow a Mother's Day Mum would never forget? What if he got Mum a fantastic card and made her the best breakfast in bed ever? In fact, if he *bought* a card, it would be much better than any home-made monstrosity Peter had painted. And, if he got up super early, he could have Mum's breakfast all ready while Peter was still snoozing. Ha! That would be the best trick ever. Henry couldn't wait to see Peter's shocked face when Peter brought up Mum's breakfast tray to find her already tucking into Henry's yummalicious treats.

'I've got a big surprise planned for you,' said Perfect Peter.

'How exciting,' said Mum, beaming.

'After all, you are the best mum in the world,' said Peter.

'Thank you, Peter,' said Mum.

Anything Peter could say, Henry could say better.

'Actually,' said Henry,

'I think you're the best mum in the universe.'

Mum smiled. 'Why, thank you, Henry,' she said.

'You're the best mum who's ever lived,' said Peter.

'You're the best mum who's ever lived and

will ever live,' said Henry.

Peter opened his mouth and then closed it. He couldn't think of anything to say to top that.

'Just wait till you see all the presents I've got you, Mum,' said Peter. 'How many do you have, Henry?'

'None of your business, worm,' said Henry. He glanced at the clock. Yikes. He only had fifteen minutes before the corner shop closed. Never mind. It was sure to be filled with fabulous Mother's Day cards and gifts.

'Be right back,' shouted Horrid Henry.

Henry stood in front of the Mother's Day card display. The shelf was empty. There wasn't a single Mother's Day card left.

How could there be no more cards?

His brilliant plan was ruined before he'd even started.

He had to find a card. If it just said, 'Best wishes' then he could write 'Happy Mother's Day' on the inside. Yikes, every card in this stupid shop cost so much. Who knew cards were so expensive?

Wait. There was a plastic box in the corner filled with cards.

ANY CARD 50 PENCE read the sign. It was his lucky day!

Shame about your Hernia

SORRY YOU'RE LEAVING

HAPPY 90TH BIRTHDAY

Henry ran over and riffled through them.

That'll do, thought Horrid Henry, grabbing the card. He'd cross out the *90th* and *birth* and write in *Mother's* instead.

She'll never notice, thought Horrid Henry.

Now, some presents. What would Mum like?

Horrid Henry wandered up the aisles.

Horrid Henry wandered down the aisles. He had three minutes left before closing time to find the best Mother's Day gifts ever.

What about a new toilet brush? This pearly white one came with a selection of cleaning supplies! And matching toilet roll holder. What a fantastic present. Mum would be sure to love it.

On the other hand, it cost £4.99. £4.99? Highway robbery. He'd already spent 50p. And he had comics to buy. He wasn't made of money.

What about a DVD, *Beat Your Blubber*? Rats, even that was £1.99. If he bought it he'd have no money left for sweets this month. Besides, Mum didn't have much blubber to beat.

Maybe *Growing Old Gracefully* would be better.

Aha. How about that book for 25p, *Hello Dentures*. The price was right, thought Horrid Henry, grabbing it. And he'd have cash left over for chocolate for him!

Hang on.

What was Mum saying she needed

just the other day? A new mop. Yes! She'd been moaning and moaning that the old one was falling apart. She'd love a new mop.

Actually, they were expensive. Rats. Why did everything cost so much? Wait. He was a genius. He'd just cut a rag into strips and then use a rubber band to attach them to the old mop handle. Voilà! A brand new mop. What mother wouldn't love such a great gift?

What a lucky mum she was, thought Horrid Henry, as he strolled home with his book and card. Now all he had to do was to dream up a few more fantastic gifts tonight, and Mother's Day was sorted. Peter was toast.

Horrid Henry sat in his bedroom. He'd made the mop. What else could he give Mum?

Why not make her some coupons?

Genius.

Another great gift for Mother's Day, and, even better, it wouldn't cost him a penny. Horrid Henry got out some paper and crayons, and wrote:

THIS MOTHERS DAY COUPON IS GOOD FOR _____

What did mums like doing best of all? Cleaning up after their children! After all, Mum was lucky to have him for her child. She could have got someone really awful, like Weepy William or Stuck-Up Steve. In fact, anyone else, really. Henry shuddered. Mum didn't know how lucky she was, having Henry for her son.

Horrid Henry filled in the coupon.

That was sure to make her happy. In fact, why not be generous, and give her a pack of ten?

There was a knock on his door.

'All ready for Mother's Day?' asked Peter.

'Of course,' said Henry smoothly. 'I've got Mum loads of presents and I'm making her breakfast in bed.'

Perfect Peter stood still.

'But that's *my* surprise,' said Peter. '*I'm* making her breakfast in bed.'

Horrid Henry smiled.

'Tough,' he said.

Peter glared at Henry.

Henry glared at Peter.

Ha, thought Horrid Henry. He'd get up super early to make sure he got Mum's breakfast ready first. He'd do soft-boiled eggs, toast, jam, juice, tea – the works.

Tee hee Peter, thought Horrid Henry. If you snooze, you lose.

Clink. Clink.

Clunk. Clunk.

Horrid Henry opened one eye. It was still dark outside. Who could be moving about the kitchen making so much noise so early?

Then Horrid Henry sat up. Peter! That little ratty toad. He'd got up early to beat Henry.

Well, not so fast.

Henry bolted out of bed and dashed into the kitchen.

There was Peter bustling around, getting out napkins and cutlery on a tray decorated with a red rose.

'Whatcha doin', worm?'

'Making Mum her Mother's Day breakfast in bed,' said Peter, placing two pieces of toast in the toaster.

'Glad someone is,' said Henry, yawning.

Peter paused.

'Aren't you making her breakfast, Henry?' asked Peter.

'Nah,' said Henry. 'You go ahead.'

Then Henry cocked his head and went to the door.

'Peter, Dad's calling you.'

'I didn't hear anything,' said Peter.

'Okay, I'll go,' said Henry. 'He said it was about Mother's Day . . .'

Peter shot out of the kitchen and dashed upstairs.

Henry nipped to the toaster.

Zip!

Peter's toast was out and in the bin.

Pop!

Horrid Henry put in FOUR pieces of toast, then stood guard.

Perfect Peter dashed back into the kitchen.

'Dad didn't call me,' said Peter. 'He was asleep.'

'Yeah he did,' said Henry.

'No, he – where's the toast I was making Mum?' said Peter.

Henry ignored him.

'Where's Mum's toast?' said Peter.

'What toast?' said Henry.

'You took my toast out of the toaster!'

'Didn't.'

'Did.'

'Didn't.'

'Liar.'

'Liar.'

Slap!

Slap!

'Mum!' screamed Henry and Peter.

'Henry slapped me,' yelled Peter.

'Peter slapped me first,' yelled Henry.

'Didn't!'

'Did!'

'Liar!'

'Liar!'

Dad stumbled in just as Henry pulled Peter's hair.

Peter started screaming.

'Henry! Leave your brother alone,' he shouted. 'It's Mother's Day.'

'I'm making her breakfast in bed, and then Peter came in and tried to steal my toast,' said Henry.

Peter gasped.

'I was making her toast first,' he wailed. 'Henry's lying.'

Dad sighed.

'Why don't you *both* make her breakfast in bed?' he said, yawning and stumbling back upstairs.

Henry looked at Peter.

Peter looked at Henry.

'Sure, Dad,' said Horrid Henry.

Henry raced to the toaster, yanked out the toast and threw it on a red tray. No time for a plate. Or butter.

Now for the eggs.

Peter snatched the jam and put it on *his* tray, then poured some juice and got out the cereal.

Oh no. Peter was getting ahead of him! He'd be first upstairs with his breakfast, and all Henry's hard work would be for nothing. Henry dashed to the fridge, snatched two eggs and flung them into egg cups. No time to soft-boil them. Anyway, they'd just be a bit runnier than normal, right?

Henry frantically poured orange juice into a glass and ran to the door with his tray. Forget the tea. Peter pounded after him, clutching his breakfast tray.

Henry shoved his tray in front of Peter, blocking him, then galloped up the stairs.

Victory!

'Happy Mother's Day,' screamed Horrid Henry, bursting into Mum and Dad's bedroom.

'Happy Mother's Day,' screamed Perfect Peter, jostling Henry as he burst into the room.

'Huunhn,' grunted Mum.

Henry tried to shove Peter out of the way with his tray.

Peter tried to shove Henry out of the way with his tray.

Slosh!

Juice went all over Henry's tray and spilled over Mum.

Cereal went all over Peter's tray and spilled over Mum.

Smash!

Crash!

Mum was covered in runny raw egg, broken shells, juice and cereal.

'Yum,' she said faintly.

'Don't worry, Mum,' yelled Horrid Henry. 'I've got just the perfect present to mop you up!'

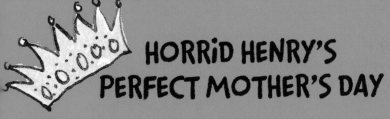

HORRID HENRY'S PERFECT MOTHER'S DAY

Mother's Day should be a day for mums
to serve their kids.

I demand:
Breakfast in bed
Chocolate for every meal
All the crisps I want
Non-stop TV
Mum to wait at my feet in case I need her
to fetch more snacks

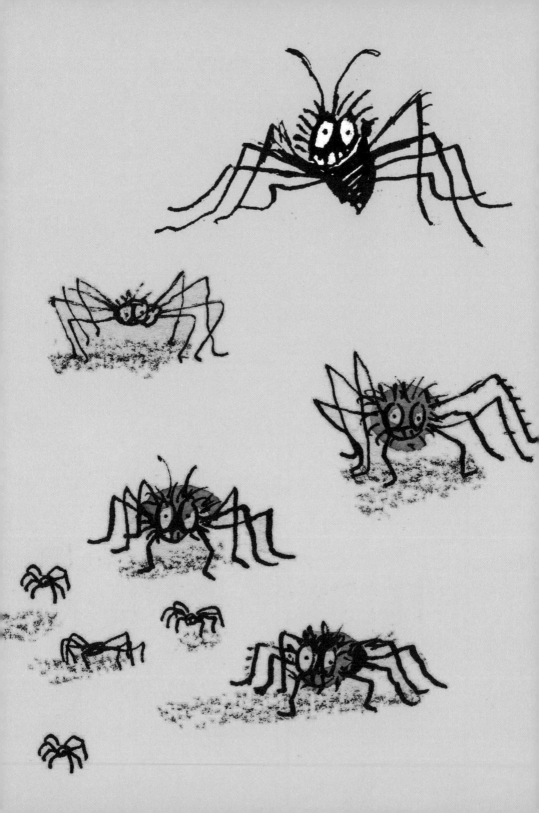

HORRID HENRY
and the Revenge of the
Bogey Babysitter

'I challenge you to a name-calling competition,' shrieked Rude Ralph. 'For the title of champion name-caller of the universe.'

Ha, thought Horrid Henry. No one knew more rude names than Henry. Not even Rude Ralph.

'You're on,' said Horrid Henry. 'Woofy.'

'Pongy.'

'Smelly.'

'Whiffy.'

'Stinky.'

'Reeky.'

'Farty.'

'Umm . . . Ummm . . .' said Ralph.

'Umm isn't a name,' crowed Henry. 'Nah Na Ne Nah Nah, I am champion.'

'Shut up, I'm thinking,' said Ralph. 'Poo breath.'

'Gloppy Goop.'

'Smellovision.'

'Odiferous.'

'Odiferous?

That's not a word,' said Ralph.

'Is too.'

'Is not.'

'Wibble pants.'

'Barf breath.'

'Turkey head.'

'Turkey head?' said Rude

Ralph.

'Turkey
head?
That's not
a—'

Ding dong.

Horrid Henry stopped jumping
up and down on Ralph's bed.

'Who's that?' said Henry.

Ralph shrugged. 'We're having a
babysitter tonight,' he said.

Horrid Henry's eyes gleamed.

A babysitter! Yeah. What could be better than a
sleepover at Ralph's with a babysitter? He'd yet to
meet one he couldn't tame. After all, he wasn't called
the Bulldozer of Babysitters for nothing. A sitter
meant hours of rampaging fun. Especially as Ralph

was bound to have one of those brilliant babysitters who let you stay up all night and eat biscuits till you were sick and watch scary movies on TV. The kind his mean, horrible parents never ever got for him.

'Great,' said Henry. 'Who?' He hoped it would be Leafy Leon. He just sat with his headphones on doing his homework. Or Allergic Alice, who he'd heard was always too busy sneezing to see kids sneaking sweets. Or maybe – oh please please please – Dippy Dora. Margaret said Dora had spent the whole evening on her phone and hadn't even noticed when Margaret stayed up past midnight and ate all the ice cream in the freezer.

'Dunno,' said Ralph. 'Mum didn't say. Probably Dora.'

Yes! thought Horrid Henry.

'And Mum's baked a chocolate fudge cake,' said Ralph.

'All for us?' said Henry.

'Nah,' said Ralph. 'Just a slice each.'

Ralph looked at Henry.

Henry looked at Ralph.

'You thinking what I'm thinking?' said Henry.

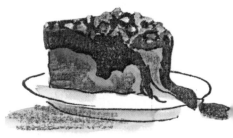

'Oh yeah,' said Ralph.

They could guzzle the whole cake and blame it on the babysitter. What brilliant luck, thought Horrid Henry. Hmm boy, he could taste that yummy, gooey scrumptious chocolate cake already.

Stomp.

Stomp.

Stomp.

There was the sound of elephants trampling.
'What was that?' said Horrid Henry.

Boom.
Boom.
Boom.

The elephants were joined by a herd of stampeding rhinoceroses.

'You don't think—' whispered Henry.
'It can't be . . .' whispered Ralph.
The walls shook.
Henry gasped.
The ground shook.
Ralph gulped.
'We'd better go and see,' said Rude Ralph.

Henry and Ralph crept down the stairs and peeked round the door.

AAARRRGHHHHHH!

Stomping towards them was the biggest, meanest, ugliest, hideously horrible teen Henry remembered from his worst nightmares. Enormous kid-mashing arms: check. Enormous spiky head: check. Enormous Henry-hating eyes and child-chewing fangs: check.

It was Rabid Rebecca, the bogey babysitter, risen from the swamp where she thrashed around with the

Loch Ness Monster and the Creature from the Black Lagoon.

'When you said you were having a babysitter, you never said it could be – Rebecca,' hissed Horrid Henry.

'I didn't know,' whimpered Rude Ralph.

'We're doomed,' moaned Horrid Henry.

'Where's the food?' bellowed Rabid Rebecca.

Ralph's mum pointed to the kitchen. 'The boys can have a small slice of cake each,' she trilled. 'Be good,' she shouted over her shoulder as she escaped.

Then Rebecca saw Henry.

Henry saw Rebecca.

'You,' said Rabid Rebecca. Her evil eyes narrowed.

'Me,' said Horrid Henry.

Last time he'd met Rabid Rebecca they'd had a fight almost to the death. Henry had hoped never to have a re-match. Then he remembered her weakness . . .

'Don't worry, she's scared of spiders,' whispered Henry.

'All we have to do is find some—'

'And don't get any ideas about spiders,' said Rebecca.

'I brought my friend Rachel. Nothing scares her.'

Horrid Henry gasped as a terrifying fiend cast a black shadow over the sitting room. Rancid Rachel was even tougher looking than Rabid Rebecca.

Rancid Rachel glared at Henry and Ralph. Her fangs gleamed.

'If I were you, I'd get straight upstairs to bed,' growled Rachel. 'That way I won't step on you by mistake.'

'But what about my chocolate cake?' squeaked Ralph. 'My mum said—'

'Our cake, you mean,' said the bogey babysitters.

'Don't you touch that cake!' squeaked Ralph.

'Yeah,' said Horrid Henry. 'Or else.'

Rancid Rachel cracked her knuckles.

'Or else what?' she snarled.

Horrid Henry took a step back.

'Ooh, doesn't that cake look yummy,' said Rachel. 'Doncha think, Becs?'

'Yeah,' said Rabid Rebecca. 'I can't wait to eat it. Nice of the brat's mum to leave it all for us. Now go to bed before we EAT . . . YOU!'

'I'm not moving,' said Horrid Henry.

'Yeah,' said Rude Ralph. 'Make me.'

'GET OUT OF HERE!' boomed the bogey babysitters, exhaling their dragon breath.

Horrid Henry and Rude Ralph sat in his bedroom. They could hear the bogey babysitters cackling and laughing in the kitchen below.

'We've got to stop them stealing all the cake,' said Ralph. 'It's not fair.'

'I know,' said Henry.

'But how?' said Ralph. 'She told us to stay in bed.'

'So what,' said Horrid Henry. He scowled. There had to be something they could do to stop the crime of the century.

'How?' said Ralph. 'Call the police?'

Tempting, thought Horrid Henry. But somehow he didn't think the police would be too keen to race over and arrest two horrible babysitters for scoffing a cake.

'We could tell Rebecca it's poisoned,' said Ralph.

'What, your mum made you a poisoned cake?' said Henry. 'Don't think they'd believe you.'

Rude Ralph hung his head.

'It's hopeless,' said Ralph. 'Now we won't get any.'

201

No cake? No yummy chocolate cake dripping with fudgy frosting and studded with sweets?

Horrid Henry wasn't the Squisher of Sitters for nothing. Wasn't there some film he'd seen, or story he'd heard, where . . . where . . .

'Get some keys and some string,' said Henry. 'And one of your dad's suits on a hanger. Hurry.'

'Why?' said Ralph.

'Do you want that cake or don't you?' said Henry. 'Now do exactly what I say.'

'AAAAARRGGGHHHH!'

The blood-curdling scream echoed through the house.

AAAAAARRRGGGGHHHHHHH!
AAAAAARRRGGGGHHHHHHH!
AAAAAARRRGGGGHHHHHHH!

Trudge.

Trudge.

Trudge.

Rabid Rebecca flung open Ralph's bedroom door. She glared at them screaming and trembling in the corner and flashed her child-chewing fangs.

'Stop screaming, you little creeps,' snarled Rabid Rebecca. 'Or I'll give you something to scream about.'

'We saw . . . we saw . . .' gasped Ralph.

'A headless ghost,' gasped Henry. 'Outside the window.'

Rabid Rebecca snorted.

'Yeah, right,' she said. 'Now shut up and go to sleep.'

She left, slamming the door behind her.

'Go!' said Horrid Henry.

Horrid Henry ran into the kitchen, panting and gasping.

There were the bogey babysitters, huddled over the cake. One slice was already gone.

Rabid Rebecca looked up, cake knife in hand.

'I smell a child,' she hissed.

'What are you doing down here?' roared Rancid Rachel. 'Go away before we . . .'

'I'm scared,' said Horrid Henry. 'I heard a noise.'

'You're just trying to make an excuse to get out of bed, you little worm,' said Rebecca.

'You'd better get out of here before I count to three,' bellowed Rachel. 'Or else.'

'There's something outside,' said Henry.

'One

Two

Thr—'

Clink.

Clink.

Clink.

The clinking noise was coming from outside the kitchen window.

'There,' whimpered Horrid Henry. He backed away.

'What was that?' said Rebecca, the cake halfway to her drooling jaws.

'Nothing,' said Rachel, shoving a huge bit in her mouth.

Clink.

Clink.

Clink.

Rachel stopped chewing.

'That,' hissed Rabid Rebecca. 'That clinking noise.'

'I told you there's something outside,' whispered Horrid Henry.

Bang.

Bang.

Bang.

Rancid Rachel stood up.
'Ahh, it's just the wind,' she said.

Bang.

Bang.

Bang.

'I'll show you,' said Rachel. 'I'm not scared.'
She marched over to the window and drew back
the curtain.

There in the dark was a headless suit, flapping and
rapping at the window.

'AAARRRGGGHHH!' screeched Rebecca. She
spat out her mouthful.

'AAARRRGGHHHH!' screeched Rachel. She
spat out her mouthful.

'It's a ghost! Hide!' they howled, racing from the
kitchen and clambering up the stairs.

'Go outside and see what it is,' screamed Horrid
Henry.

'No way,' shrieked Rebecca.

They barricaded themselves into the
bathroom and locked the door.

Horrid Henry snatched the
cake off the cake stand and
raced back to Ralph's
room.

Ralph was standing
at the open window,
dangling a hanger from a
string with his dad's suit on
it.

Henry beamed at Ralph as
he hauled in the suit and untied
the keys he'd used to clink on the
ground.

Ralph beamed at Henry.

'Good job, partner,' said
Henry, helping himself to a
gigantic piece of chocolate
cake. Hmmm boy, it was
delicious.

'Good job, partner,' said
Ralph, digging into an even
bigger one.

'Won't your mum
be furious with Rebecca

when she comes home and finds all the cake gone?' mumbled Henry, taking another enormous slice.

'Boy will she ever,' said Ralph. 'I bet Rebecca never babysits here again.'

HENRY'S BEST BABYSITTER RULES

1. **Must** let children stay up as late as they want

2. **Must** let children watch scary movies

3. Children to control the TV remote

4. Unlimited ice cream and sweets

5. All younger brothers and sisters sent to bed IMMEDIATELY

HORRID HENRY'S FILM FINALE: THE ENEMY ENDINGS

So long, Suckers! It was horrible knowing you!

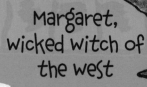

Margaret, wicked witch of the west

Godzilla in 'Bye-Bye Boudicca'

CALLING ALL
BOOK LOVERS!

Sign up online for the latest news
about all of your favourite authors,
as well as upcoming events,
exclusive competitions and lots of fun extras!

Visit
www.orionchildrensbooks.co.uk
for more information

Horrid Henry Books

Storybooks

Horrid Henry

Horrid Henry and the Secret Club

Horrid Henry Tricks the Tooth Fairy

Horrid Henry's Nits

Horrid Henry Gets Rich Quick

Horrid Henry's Haunted House

Horrid Henry and the Mummy's Curse

Horrid Henry's Revenge

Horrid Henry and the Bogey Babysitter

Horrid Henry's Stinkbomb

Horrid Henry's Underpants

Horrid Henry Meets the Queen

Horrid Henry and the Mega-Mean Time Machine

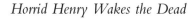

Early Readers

Don't be Horrid Henry

Horrid Henry's Birthday Party

Horrid Henry's Holiday

Horrid Henry's Underpants

Horrid Henry Gets Rich Quick

Horrid Henry and the Football Fiend

Horrid Henry's Nits

Horrid Henry and Moody Margaret

Horrid Henry's Thank You Letter

Horrid Henry Car Journey

Moody Margaret's School

Horrid Henry's Tricks and Treats

Horrid Henry's Rainy Day

Horrid Henry's Author Visit

Horrid Henry Meets the Queen

Horrid Henry's Sports Day

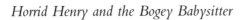

Colour books

Joke Books

Horrid Henry's Joke Book

Horrid Henry's Jolly Joke Book

Horrid Henry's Mighty Joke Book

Horrid Henry versus Moody Margaret

Horrid Henry's Hilariously Horrid Joke Book

Horrid Henry's Purple Hand Gang Joke Book

Horrid Henry's All Time Favourite Joke Book

Horrid Henry's Jumbo Joke Book

Activity Books

Horrid Henry's Brainbusters

Horrid Henry's Headscratchers

Horrid Henry's Mindbenders

Horrid Henry's Colouring Book

Horrid Henry's Puzzle Book

Horrid Henry's Sticker Book

Horrid Henry Runs Riot

Horrid Henry's Annual 2015

Horrid Henry's Classroom Chaos

Horrid Henry's Holiday Havoc

Horrid Henry's Wicked Wordsearches

Horrid Henry's Mad Mazes

Horrid Henry's Crazy Crosswords

Fact Books

Horrid Henry's Ghosts

Horrid Henry's Dinosaurs

Horrid Henry's Sports

Horrid Henry's Food

Horrid Henry's King and Queens

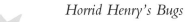

Horrid Henry's Bugs

Horrid Henry's Animals

Horrid Henry's Ghosts

Horrid Henry's Crazy Creatures

Visit Horrid Henry's website at
www.horridhenry.co.uk for competitions,
games, downloads and a monthly newsletter